Arthur Christopher Benson

William Laud, sometime archbishop of Canterbury

A Study by Arthur Christopher Benson

Arthur Christopher Benson

William Laud, sometime archbishop of Canterbury
A Study by Arthur Christopher Benson

ISBN/EAN: 9783337261733

Printed in Europe, USA, Canada, Australia, Japan

Cover: Foto ©Andreas Hilbeck / pixelio.de

More available books at **www.hansebooks.com**

ARCHBISHOP LAUD

A STUDY

"Et levavi oculos meos, et vidi ; et ecce vir, et in manu ejus funiculus mensorum.

"Et dixi: Quo tu vadis? Et dixit ad me, Ut metiar Jerusalem, et videam quanta sit latitudo ejus, et quanta longitudo ejus."—ZACH. PROPH. ii. 1, 2.

WILLIAM LAUD

SOMETIME

ARCHBISHOP OF CANTERBURY

A STUDY

BY

ARTHUR CHRISTOPHER BENSON, B.A.

SCHOLAR OF KING'S COLLEGE, CAMBRIDGE; ASSISTANT MASTER
AT ETON COLLEGE

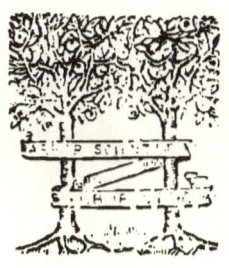

LONDON

KEGAN PAUL, TRENCH & CO., 1, PATERNOSTER SQUARE

1887

TO MY FATHER

THIS SLIGHT MEMORIAL

OF ONE OF HIS PREDECESSORS

IS WITH ALL LOVE AND REVERENT AFFECTION

DUTIFULLY DEDICATED.

PREFACE.

Two reasons induced me to try and sketch the life of Laud. The first was that it has been customary to take an extravagant view of him—either to set him forward as the champion of all that is traditional and venerable in Church doctrine or discipline, the type of the moderate High Churchman, with a clearly defined position neither Romanist nor Lutheran ; or, on the other hand, to decry him as an obstinate bigot, self-willed and important, who fell a victim to his own intolerant prejudices. Neither of these seemed to me a fair or worthy view : he was certainly not the latter, he was far from being the former ; he holds an intermediate position. I have not endeavoured to make him into a hero or a saint, but to depict him as a man of an undaunted spirit, of an inflexible if not heroic mould, as one of the most vivid and interesting figures in the very centre of one of the most gigantic tragedies that has ever been played out on the stage of English history.

And in the second place, living in the house which is so closely connected with him, being often brought into contact with some little memorial of him, talking beneath his portrait, worshipping beneath his chapel screen, seeing his signature written in the stiff tall hand, all this created a strong wish to try and realize, as he moved and spoke and looked, one of the most definite personalities that has ever occupied the chair of St. Augustine.

Few people have received so much damage from their defenders as Laud. His apologists, not content with making much out of the amiable features of his character, have not only slurred over a great deal that is undeniably unamiable, but have in many cases endeavoured to put a favourable construction on what is harsh and unpleasing, and should have been otherwise. Thus they have succeeded in producing a portrait that we feel at once to be exaggerated and disproportionate, and not even lifelike. He has been damned with praise.

Now, Laud's was a vehement, almost violent character, and there was much that was angular and disagreeable about him. Offensive peculiarities in a great man have often their humorous side ; and that, combined with the natural veneration which the biographer feels, or grows to feel, may, as in the case of Boswell's " Johnson," produce a delightful result. But it must not be done deliberately. The picture must be made complete, and framed, and hung; and others must be left to judge whether they can love the original well enough to condone his uglinesses.

First comes Heylyn—Peter Heylyn, chaplain to the Archbishop, and, after the Restoration, Subdean of Westminster. He is Laud's Boswell. His biography—" Cyprianus Anglicanus," as he calls it, for Cyprian was a decapitated prelate—is very nearly a first-rate book. It is racy, humorous, vivid, and affectionate ; but it is portentously long, and has no index. No one but a student would read it now.

But to Heylyn every biographer of Laud must be deeply indebted. Again and again he must be quoted. He is sometimes, I think, sublime. The death scene is a noble piece of writing. I have given it in full.

I subjoin here, as most appropriate, Heylyn's own account of his first interview with the Archbishop. It is a good specimen of his style ; and it will give the reader a good idea of the character of the man, his pomposity, his complacency, and his zeal for his patron.

"The Archbishop," he writes, "being kept to his chamber at the time with lameness, I had both the happiness of being taken into his special knowledge of me, and the opportunity of a longer conference than I should otherwise have expected. I went to present my service to him, as he was preparing for this journey, and was appointed to attend him the same day seven-night, when I might presume on his return.

"Coming precisely at the time, I heard of his mischance, and that he kept himself to his chamber; but order had been left among his servants that if I came he should be made acquainted with it, which being done accordingly, I was brought into his chamber, where I found him sitting on a chair with his lame leg resting on a pillow. Commanding that nobody should come and interrupt him till he called for them, he caused me to sit down by him, and inquired first into the course of my studies, which he well approved of, exhorting me to hold myself in that moderate course in which he found me. He fell afterwards to discourse of some passages in Oxford in which I was specially concerned, and told me thereupon the story of such opposition as had been made against him in the University by Archbishop Abbot and others, and encouraged me not to shrink if I had already found and should hereafter find the like. I was with him thus *remotis arbitris*, almost two hours. It grew almost twelve of the clock, and then he knocked for his servants to come to him ; he dined that day in his ordinary dining-room, which was the first time he had done so since his mishap. He caused me to tarry dinner with him, and used me with no small respect, which was much noticed by some gentlemen (Elphinstone, one of his Majesty's cupbearers being one of the company) who dined that day with him. A passage, I confess, not pertinent to my present story."

Next must be mentioned Le Bas, who wrote a life in 1840. He was a Fellow of Trinity, and afterwards Principal of the East India College at Haileybury. He did a good deal of theological work, such as the life of Cranmer and the Wyclif movement,—lively writing enough, though superseded now.

Thus there is a gap of two hundred years between the two biographers. During that period Laud was accepted and forgotten. With the Oxford movement was felt considerable curiosity as to the life and character of a man so sympathetically inclined to the Ritualistic creed, a man, it was said, of so primitive a mould, the staunch upholder of Church tradition and authority. Le Bas was a man of original mind ; his book is brisk and suggestive : but he did not explore ; he is inaccurate and not well-proportioned.

Dean Hook's is a good working biography, not original or high in tone, but a worthy portrait in a sound series.

Professor Mozley's essay on Laud is perhaps the best known of his studies, and the liveliest life of the man. It is delightful reading ; but the more one knows of Laud, the deeper is the distrust one feels of that brilliant paradoxical style. Mozley is too imaginative and enthusiastic ; he builds too much on small things ; there is too strong a personal factor throughout. Deep as is the debt which writers on Laud must owe to his book, much as I owe him in the way of kindled interest and sympathetic enlightenment, I cannot help recording the fact that it is a portrait reminding one every now and then, by a clever trick, by a sympathetic gesture, of the original, but a deceitful portrait after all. There is no book I would more confidently recommend to a would-be student of Laud and his life ; there is no book I should be more surprised at a genuine student's accepting and retaining.

Of incidental portraiture, Professor Gardiner's stands at the other end of the scale—Laud steps on to the scene at intervals in the whole drama of the Rebellion : but Professor Gardiner's portraits, if the criticism is not presumptuous, are hardly lively enough ; he is amazingly correct and cautious, and satisfies without pleasing.   Charles, Strafford, Pym, —it is always the same—not one of them carries the reader away.

I have also studied carefully such books as Clarendon's History, the "Rushworth Papers," the "Eikon Basilike," Aubrey's Letters, and many other histories and collections, for contemporary portraits and records of contemporary affairs. And I have had free access to the Lambeth papers, which contain many curious points, many delightful confirmations, too minute to enter into larger histories, but which I have endeavoured to embody in this little study of a character and a life.   Historians have been before me ; the papers have been ransacked many times.   But it is the privilege of the biographer, who works on a more microscopic scale, to emphasize and drag to light all kinds of tiny relics, little papers annotated by friendly hands, flotsam and jetsam of the ages that accumulated fortuitously in muniment cupboards and archive chambers.   Whether or not such search and such treasure-trove can give satisfaction to others remains to be seen.   I can genuinely say that to me it has been a labour of love—a labour in which my interest and delight have never flagged —a task to which I have returned in hour after hour of leisure, in a life full of little interruptions, and never found irksome, or dreary, or dull.

I must, in conclusion, record my great obligation to my friend, Mr. W. H. D. Boyle, who has throughout corrected the following pages, and suggested many improvements.

A. C. B.

Eton,
   July, 1887.

ARCHBISHOP LAUD.

INTRODUCTORY.

IT is impossible to pursue the history of a single life upon chronological lines, unless it is made a mere chronology. A single trait has sometimes to be pursued into remote events, and then to be recalled into stricter temporal sequence. I think, therefore, it will be as well first to tabulate several historical events, in themselves not unfamiliar, but whose exact relative position is perhaps undecided, except in the minds of specialists; so that if I have to treat historical events unchronologically, it may be clear that I do so, not because they are not chronologically related, but because some events have a more direct connection with primary causes than other events which preceded them in point of actual occurrence. A knowledge of dates is not a knowledge of history.

B

Laud born ...	1573
James I. succeeded ...	1603
Laud President of St. John's, Oxford ...	1611
Proposal for Spanish Marriage ...	1615
Laud Bishop of St. David's ...	1621
The Spanish Journey ...	1624
Charles I. succeeded ...	1625
Murder of Buckingham ; Laud Bishop of London	1628
Strafford Lord Deputy of Ireland ...	1631
Laud Archbishop of Canterbury ...	1633
Scottish Prayer Book ...	1636
Hampden's Trial ended ...	1637
Scottish Covenant ...	1638
Short and Long Parliament ; Laud in the Tower	1640
Execution of Strafford...	1641
Edgehill ...	1642
Marston Moor ; Naseby ; Laud executed ...	1644
Execution of Charles I. ...	1649

To the amateur historian the period of the Stuarts is wonderfully attractive : it is so accessible. In any old-fashioned library he can find contemporary literature in abundance ; he may skim through pamphlets, sermons, letters, tractates, in their antique brown type, on stiff wrinkled paper— sermons that seem formal and affected now, but that made ears tingle then ; letters that kindled rebellion, and tractates that fanned it into flame. He can get somewhat of what these people thought themselves ; he need not take it second-hand : or if he prefers to do so—if he mistrusts his own judgment—he has several competent historians, working from adequate material, from whom he may select his favourite. Their conclusions may be fanciful, but, at any rate, they are conclusions. One historian may suppress documents, another may distort them,—but the documents are there. It is not like the history, of which there is so much in our hands, where both facts and conclusions are hypothetical.

The period of the Stuarts is so refreshing a contrast to earlier English history, to the childish directness which characterizes the portraits of earlier leaders and kings. Now and then, it is true, a real character peeps out. Henry II., biting the rushes as he rolls on the floor in rage, or, as in the Vita Magna of St. Hugh, stitching up his torn finger, like his grandfather, the glover,—this is a real man. Abbot Samson is a real man. In Shakespeare, too, princes and cardinals are real men, though not the real ones ; they have a flavour of antiquity about them. But for most of us John is all wicked and Henry III. all weak ; Richard III. all hump and hypocrisy ; Henry VI. a melancholy pietist, with an interest in education. And even if a certain definiteness does attach itself to the characters of the kings, how hopelessly impersonal the lesser lights are apt to be ! A biographer of the Black Prince has nothing to tell us. The Earls Edwin and Morcar are proverbial for being dry.

Simon de Montfort is little better than an elegant shadow. Wyclif and Wykeham are nothing but venerable names. As we get down to Henry VIII. the mist clears a little, thanks to Lord Herbert and Strype. There is some flesh and blood about him. Elizabeth is a little phantasmal from her pomp and her wardrobes ; but James I., the coarse pedant— here is a man at last.

And Charles, he is a human being too,—so truthfully inconsistent, so far stranger than fiction, from the day when he first said merrily to his boy-friends at dinner that he could never have been a lawyer, *for he could not defend a bad nor yield in a good cause,* to the day when, all in black, dazed with fright and desperate dignity, he spoke, and spoke those poor rambling incoherent words before the windows of his own hall—words which, like the ravings of delirium, give the reader a thrill of horror even now.

" We have the misfortune," Strafford said to Laud, " to serve a gracious prince that knows not how to be, or to be made great."

This clever sentence contains epigrammatically a rapid outline of the character of this unfortunate king—at least for those who have any sympathy with him and his position. He was, above all things, to those who served and loved him a gracious prince. There was something fascinating about him. Strafford and Laud were enamoured, not of the monarch, but of the monarchy; but it is certain that they would never have given the same passionate devotion to the service of the throne had it been occupied by Charles's father, or by either of Charles's sons, or, indeed, by any but Charles himself. He was, in fact, a man born to be king; there was something kingly in the nature, inbred, not only developed by circumstances.

In the first place, there was a singular chastity about the man in a court that was not chaste. Perfect chastity is a rare and precious jewel among the crowns of our English kings; the temptations of sense are so numerous, and the ease in compassing any desire so absolute. But the white coronation robe which Charles, alone of our kings, chose for himself, rejecting the customary purple, as a sign of the "virgin purity in which he came to be espoused to his people," was no mere ideal allegory; it truly symbolized his unstained nature.

For the rest, he was of a grimly obstinate nature, of a stubbornness partly innate and partly fostered by his position, which not only never gave way, but never even saw that it was right or politic to give way. How it has come about that the commonest view of Charles is that of a weak, religious, melancholy and romantic man is impossible to conceive—from his portrait probably, and nothing else.

I hope that incidental touches throughout this volume will illustrate this view of his character. He will never be found to be weak, save perhaps in the case of Strafford's death ; he was religious, but in no sense sentimental, almost as sternly practical as Laud himself, and taking an even more decidedly Erastian view of the Church as a great State engine for securing obedience and right thought ; he became melancholy as he found himself swept gradually off his feet by the tide which he could not stem and to which he would not yield ; romantic in one sense he was, if to be romantic is to be unfortunate, and to have the power of attaching to oneself, by character and circumstances, some of the most ardent if not the noblest spirits of the land. So he moved in his dignified wilfulness through life, often stirring the reader's pity, even his anger, but never contemptible, never not a king.

But he bore one blemish that was deep indeed. At crises of his life, and at anxious moments of the national history, a fatal characteristic appeared : a curious moral obliquity came out—faithlessness, as Macaulay calls it, an utter inability to keep to his word. Still, it must be allowed that this, too, was rather the result of his idea of monarchical prerogative than a deliberate desertion of principle, a lack of rectitude. He could not bring himself to feel instinctively that a bargain was as much a bargain, a promise as much a promise, when made between king and people as between gentleman and gentleman. In the smaller field of domestic and private life Charles was acutely sensitive about such things as honour and the sacredness of the pledged word ; but as soon as the scene shifted to the wider arena of politics, he seemed to forget that the principles of morality were every bit as true in that less visible atmosphere.

If the king make a promise, he may also disregard it ; no promise can be binding on him which, at a later date, he may think it right to violate ;—thus fatally he argued, not, we must believe, from moral blindness, but from false and stolid pride.

CHAPTER I.

AT Lambeth, in the guard-room still so-called, now
dining-room, where the portraits of the Archbishops
hang, immediately opposite the door by which you
enter, and close to a window, so that the yellow
London light falls on it, hangs a portrait that instantly attracts the attention.   True, it is a master-
piece of Vandyck's; but it is not the painting
that surprises, though it is to its utter life-likeness
that the surprise is due.   Again and again I have
heard people ask, " And who is that very extraor-
dinary-looking person?" and, on being told who it
is, say in a tone of incredulous bewilderment, "*That*
Laud!"

The fact is that the name of Laud, to those to
whom it conveys any ideas at all, stands for one
of two things: either he is a type of all that is
sacerdotal and objectionable in the Church of England, the most mischievous prelate that has ever
borne supreme rule there; he is the bigot, the

ecclesiastic, *par excellence*,—the eternal instance of
what is called the "clerical" mind—using the word
in the sense of narrow, sectarian, credulous, and
unsympathetic.   And these are astonished, for he
wears the face of a kindly cheery man.   Or else he
is the "martyred Laud," the saviour of the Church
in her Catholic aspect, the restorer of the shrine,
the true son of Aaron, robed as God Himself ap-
points.   And the face bears witness to none of
these things ; if faces betray character this man
had little of the saint about him.

Of all the thirty-four portraits of ecclesiastics who
there appear, this one is the most enigmatic.   It
represents a man in a square cap, worn very far
back on the head so as to show a great height of
forehead.   The face is plump and short, with but
few lines in it, of a fine fresh colour.   He was then
some sixty-seven years of age, and he looks but
forty.   The little moustache and imperial worn by
the clergy of that date give a curiously secular finish
to what is already a secular face.   But the most
marked features are the small, delicately pencilled
eyebrows, drawn very high up by the wrinkling of
the brows, giving a look of half-cynical surprise, a
mute protest, to the face.   Downdropped brows, like
a penthouse over receding eyes, give either a pen-
sive or a gloomy secretive look : of this there is

absolutely no trace in Laud's face. The whole expression would be called sunny, if it were not for that half-pathetic, half-humorous raising of the brow. They seem to say, " I have told you ; I have warned you. I have laid down before you the paths you ought to walk in, the paths you ought to tread ; if you will not be warned you may walk on still in darkness, you may go your own way,— I at least have done my part."

It is not trivial to contrast Laud's portrait with that of his master, Charles Stuart himself. The contrast is a painful one. The look of serene prosperity about the prelate loses ground by the side of the gloom and weariness in the face of the king—that look of doom, as it has been called—that has won him, and will win him, so many passionate admirers.

The window by which Laud hangs looks into the front court of the Palace—gravelled now, a grass-grown lawn then. The air is full of the solemn roar of London. To the left is the great gate which the rioters assaulted ; to the right, the skeletons of the high garden elms under which he walked with Hales of Eton. Close below the windows of the library, in spite of London fog and sunless air, flourish the broad-fingered, grey-green leaves of the fig-trees, the successors of those that he himself planted, by which he used to pace ;

where, he records in his diary, at the first touch
of spring, his tortoise, then some sixty years old,
that had been given him when at Oxford, used
to issue from some secret crack and crawl painfully
about. And, curiously enough, when the other day
I was turning over some dusty relics—old parch-
ment-deeds, faded stiff church-vestments, seals and
crosses, that repose in an oak press in the Muni-
ment-room,—there I came upon a tortoise-shell at
the back of the shelf, on which was pasted a strip
of paper, inscribed in antique brown characters,
"The Shell of a Tortoise, which was put into the
Garden at Lambeth in the year 1633, where it
remained till the year 1753, when it was unfortunately (or mortally) killed by the overflowing
of the river." *

Laud was born at Reading, a town he always
loved. His memory was long held in honour there.
A minute in the Corporation Diary, in 1695, records
the decision that a small oak desk should be affixed
to the panelling on the left side of the Council-
Chamber chimney-piece, and that a copy of the
"Troubles and Tryal of William Laud" should be
chained to the desk with a chain of brass for ever.
The house where he was born has disappeared, but

---

* Or perhaps, as Ducarel says, "the negligence of the gardener."
The slip is nearly illegible.

the fact is commemorated by the nomenclature of the block that has succeeded it—Laud Place.

In Reading he built an almshouse, which still exists, endowing it with lands at Bray. "*Done*," he writes, with characteristic method, against the project in the little paper of " Things I have projected to do if God bless me in them." There is another curious and characteristic entry about that project, in the Diary : " The way to do the town of Reading good, for their poor ; which may be compassed by God's blessing upon me, though my wealth be small. And I hope God will bless me in it, because it was His own motion in me. For this way never came into my thoughts (though I had much beaten about it) till this night, as I was at my prayers. Jan. 1, 1633–4."

He was of the middle class—a class which the Puritans introduced to importance : they had been overlooked till then. He was the only child of a second marriage. His father was a well-to-do master tailor, employing many work-people, and leaving a good report behind him. " E fæce plebis," said his enemies—" Raked out of the dunghill." His maternal uncle, Sir Benjamin Webb, had been Lord Mayor of London. There was no trouble in the family from poverty.

This origin must be kept in mind. It is sometimes supposed that he sided with the party of aristocratic instincts against democratic tendencies ; if he did, it was because the former represented tradition, authority, rule, as against freedom, independence, self-government. No man ever had fewer aristocratic sympathies. Men of low origin rising to great positions are often unduly dazzled and impressed by the atmosphere in which they find themselves. Laud was neither dazzled nor impressed ; he had not a touch of meanness in his composition. He had a keen eye for men of weight—the King, Buckingham, Strafford,—these were great influential factors in politics, and Laud gravitated to them ; but for birth and position he had no sort of respect. One of the reasons why he made such universal enemies—enemies in every class and every rank—was that he heeded distinctions so little; whether the offender was earl or barber, if he offended he must suffer. He was hard on the people, and they hated him ; he was hard on the nobility, and they would not protect him. His origin was constantly made the subject of taunt and ridicule in later life. Heylyn describes how he found him walking in his garden, looking troubled at a lampoon that he had found on the walk, flung over the wall ; not so much at the fact that he had not, as he said, the good fortune

to be born a gentleman, as at the virulence and ill-
feeling that such an attack betokened ; and it is
evident that he was very genuinely pleased with
Heylyn's apt and humorous quotation, of a certain
pope who said of himself that he was " illustri domo
natus," *i.e.* a broken-down shed that let in the light.
Laud's morbid sensibility to libels and lampoons is
among the most curious traits of his character : his
entries in the Diary on the receipt of one of them
became pathetic and soft to a strange degree in a
man of so flinty a purpose. But this is a side issue.
It must be borne in mind that he was of ordinary
burgher origin, brought up in middle-class traditions. However, his education began early, his
home traditions were probably never very strong,
and he was never married—that is to say, he had
none of the temptations to the domestic point-of-
view, which is so characteristic of the English
middle-class.

In the first entry in the Diary occur the words,
" In my infancy I was in danger of death by sickness." In 1596 the only entry is, " I had a great
sickness." In 1597 the only entry is, " And another."
And it is so all along. In 1619, he " falls suddenly
dead for a long time at Wycombe ; " he is taken
ill in his coach ; he has a very " fierce salt rheum
in the left eye that almost endangers it ; " " became

suddenly lame, whether through some humour falling down upon my left leg, or through the biting
of bugs, I know not." The Diary is full of these,
almost as full as George Eliot's. But Laud never
diagnoses his sensations. I think it is important
to keep this knowledge in our minds about him ;
neither his portrait nor his public acts would betray
it. He never broke down ; he never took a
holiday ; he never took any exercise. A public
man is even censured nowadays if he does not take
a respite from his official labours, and refresh the
jaded brain with sea or glacier air. Laud never
left England. There is little trace of his having
left his work, and this when, besides being a very
active Archbishop—not, however, with the care of
the colonial Churches—he was also Prime Minister
and President of the Board of Trade, with a seat
on the Foreign Committee, besides discharging
spontaneously year after year for Oxford and
Dublin Universities, in his capacity as Chancellor,
duties which whiten the hairs of Heads of houses
when undertaken most unwillingly for a period
of two years. The fact was that Laud, like his
friend and ally Strafford, was possessed of what
has been well called an obstinate indoors constitution. He was never well, never incapacitated.
A week after breaking a sinew of his leg he

officiated at the marriage of the Duke of Buckingham's daughter.

Constant ill-health with conscientious strong-
willed people seems to act as a perpetual stimulus
to action. On gentler meditative souls it sometimes
traces gracious saintly lines; but not on men of
tougher fibre—they need the counter-irritation of
work and life, otherwise they chafe and writhe. If
they get work, they take it greedily; they do not
become valetudinarians; they do not succumb;
they busy themselves in details, and thus contrive
to stifle the constant feeling of uneasiness: at the
same time it keeps them alive to graver questions.
Invalids are generally idealists. When, on the
other hand, men of superb physique and super-
abundant vigour find themselves at a great centre,
they are apt to fritter themselves away upon
material surroundings and absorbing attention to
details. Absorption in details was a temptation of
Laud's, too; but the pressure of malaise kept him
from losing himself in fancied effectiveness; he
kept his principles in view. No doubt his principles
erred on the side of being too material, but they
were principles; he worked not by the impulse of
the moment, but on certain deliberate lines.

CHAPTER II.

" I HAD the happiness," Laud says, "to be educated under a very severe schoolmaster." He was
also a perceptive one ; he said of the boy, just as
it has probably been said of dozens of clever lads
who never do emerge to greatness, that he would
make a name some day. His high spirit, his quick
apprehension, and, curiously enough, the strange
stuff of his dreams, aroused great expectations.
" When you are a little great person," said this
austere tutor, alluding to Laud's stature, "I hope you
will remember Reading school." The boy's industry,
in spite of his invalid constitution, was very great ;
and there was a curious solidity of judgment and
quiet independence of temper noted even in those
early days. At sixteen he went to Oxford, to
St. John's, a humble pile of mottled flint and gray
stone ; its stately garden front and academic grove
were of Laud's own later contriving. A year after
his admission he was chosen scholar, partly on

C

his abilities, partly, it is said, out of respect to the
memory of his father, the Mayor of Reading
having the nomination for that turn.

It is an interesting fact, perhaps not more, that
Laud's tutor at St. John's—that is to say, the man
to whose teaching and care he was absolutely
committed at a most impressionable age—was John
Buckeridge, afterwards Bishop of Rochester, and
later, through his pupil's influence, of Ely. He
was, perhaps, the leading controversialist in sacra-
mental matters, and upheld the lowly kneeling to
receive the sacred elements as a matter both of
tradition and natural feeling. It is not probable
that Laud had up to this time enjoyed any particularly ecclesiastical conversation. He was, of
course, intended for the Church. Most ambitious
young men, of the middle and lower orders, who
meant to rise, did so through the Church ; the Bar
was not the ladder to advancement that it is now.
Laud must have been all along, by his most instinctive and deepest promptings, a churchman, an
ecclesiastic; and his High Church, Traditional, even
Arminian tendencies were natural to him :—but
it is not mere fancy, I think, to attribute to this
early influence the bent which was so decided
afterwards ; he probably made his first entry into
the ecclesiastical world of controversy and discus-

sion at this point. Buckeridge would be sure to have talked the altar controversy over with his pupils, especially with so eager and sympathetic a listener as Laud ; and it is not improbable that to this early bias his later strength of feeling on the subject is due. It probably then assumed undue proportions in his mind, and never quite lost them.

At the age of twenty he was made a Fellow. At this time the atmosphere of Oxford was charged with Calvinism. Abbot, Master of University, Laud's predecessor at Canterbury, was the ruling spirit.* Laud, one against a host—for he had hardly a single sympathizer—detested not only their doctrines but their accessories. It was characteristic of that gloomy superstition to override all the more pleasing ornaments of worship, all the beauty of holiness—music was worldly and architecture distracting. " No whistling in church," said Glover, as the great organ at Ely came down. They forgot that the capacity for beauty in natural things was, after all, God's work as well. It escaped

---

* His favourite tenet was the descent of the visible Church, not through the main unmistakable channel, but through by-waters and side-streams. That a man should have gravely held the truth to have passed through Berengarians, Albigenses, Wicklifites, Hussites, to Luther and Calvin, is nearly incredible ; yet this was the text of Abbot.

them that when they cried for the Bible and nothing but the Bible, all they meant was texts which they had themselves selected. Lectures and homilies, sermons and discourses, extempore prayer, broken only by grim psalm-singing, went near to eclipse the delicate fabric of Church worship that had attracted their forefathers, and that Laud loved with a consuming love : " The zeal of Thine house hath even eaten me," he said.

It seems, however, that Laud did not so much despise the directness and ugliness of these Bible Christians, as hate their rashness and temerity in dealing with the class of subjects over which they loved to linger—Reprobation and the bondage of the Will. Calvinism bore the same relation to the religion of the day that militant agnosticism and scientific unbelief bear to it now. Calvinism was free thought—the rationalizing of religion on biblical lines. Laud loved authority ; he had the Roman instinct of sternly forbidding the by-paths of speculative thought to ordinary minds. And to unenlightened wavering souls such speculation is beset with dangers ; submission is the more prac-ticable way. All along it is evident that Laud's battle was fought against free speculation ; and when we see him pitted against Calvinism we are apt to forget this—we are inclined to treat it

as a purely ecclesiastical contest, circulating about
the washing of pots and cups and the furniture
of the sanctuary. But the altar controversy, to
which I shall have to allude, was only the symbol
of a far deeper schism, where Laud was fighting
for authority and tradition, and his enemies for
liberty of practice. The arena has opened so
much lately. It is religion against, not irreligion,
but non-religion now. Then it was a more
intestine warfare, but the interests involved were
the same. We are prone, too, to feel that
men like Laud, with strong feelings about the
Divine right of kings and the authority of the
Church, must have been of the party which we
call by the name of Tory. But this is not the
case. At Oxford, in the midst of this Calvinistic
school, he appeared as the daring innovator
against all the prejudices of the day. He was
described by the leaders of University thought in
the terms in which we should describe a fanatical
Radical : though the tyranny for which he strove
was retrograde in their eyes. In fact, it was
the tyranny over thought that he aimed at—
Calvinism was the tyranny in thought.

The altar controversy deserves a special consideration at this point, from the important place
which it holds in the disputes of the time. It is

a controversy which falls peculiarly under the derision of the unsympathetic mind. The man who takes what he calls an unprejudiced view of history,—which may be more properly called an ignorant view,—finds great matter of mirth in the fact that a nation should be divided over the position of the Communion table in church. "They could not really care," he says. He is inclined to relegate it to the same category of controversies as that which agitated Lilliput—at which end to open an egg. But it is always so : strife rages most fiercely when mere details are the matters of dispute. We are as little free from it now as ever. Is not the position of the Priest at the altar an unworthy matter to make good men enemies?

The facts are shortly these. The Elizabethan rubric was all for convenience. The table was to stand where it had stood at times when it was not wanted for use. At celebrations it was to be moved to the centre of the church or chancel, wherever the minister could be most conveniently seen and heard, and where general access to the table was easiest.

But the table was heavy, and sacristans are seldom known to err on the side of physical activity. The table was moved to the centre of the church, and there it stayed. In cathedrals and

private chapels it remained, as a rule, at the east.
Then began the Puritan revival. The Communion,
the mystic, super-rational, direct union of the
believer's soul with his Lord, the sacrament of
spirituality, was thrust out. The pure Word, or
rather diluted extracts of the Word, took its place ;
pulpit and reading-desk were glorified. The
Shechinah migrated there. The altar became
a convenient table, a depository for the accidents
of a mere commemoration.

Had matters remained at this point, no dispute
need have arisen ; but this degraded table was
treated with gross irreverence—schoolboys laid
their satchels, farmers their hats and sticks upon
it. The churchwardens made up their accounts
on it ; it was even put to lower uses by plumbers
and glaziers. The Puritans would have it that it
was common and unclean.

When Laud, as Archbishop, summarily ordered
it to be placed altarwise at the east, railed in by
the *cancelli*, which had given their name to the
chancel, the Puritans saw in it a deliberate attempt
to restore a hated doctrine. And it was a deliberate attempt. Laud's view of the Sacrament was
much what a moderate High Churchman would
hold now. He felt it to be the crown and con-
summation of Christian mysteries ; to stand at the

head of the scheme ; to impart the Divine union
for which the teaching of desk and pulpit prepared
and fitted a devout soul. The Puritans, who held
it to be merely a commendable practice which
every man who was at heart devoted to the Word
would be glad to continue, saw the old tyranny
of the Church rehabilitated by this assertion.

Laud was Fellow of St. John's for ten years.
During the whole of this time his character was
maturing ; but he was himself all along. He knew
the precise extent and limits of his own beliefs ;
he never lost an opportunity of recommending
them. Whenever he got an opportunity he stepped
forward, explained and justified some obnoxious
doctrine : now Baptismal Regeneration, now Apos-
tolical Succession through the Church of Rome.
On one occasion he was actually cited before the
Vice-Chancellor, to answer to a charge of heresy.
And here he behaved most characteristically : he
did not defy, or prophesy, or make a meek submission ; he gravely refuted the charge, step by
step, coldly and courteously, and was dismissed.
Abbot hated him ; and Abbot was Oxford then.
" It was a heresy," Laud writes, " to be seen in my
company, to salute me in the street." A sermon
was preached against him at St. Mary's, in his
presence.

"Might not Christ say," cried Mr. Robert Abbot, brother of the Vice-Chancellor, from the University pulpit, pale with passion, and staring at Laud, where he sat among the masters—"Might not Christ say, 'What art thou? Romish or English? Papist or Protestant? Or what art thou? a mongrel, or compound of both?—a Protestant by ordination; a Papist in point of free will and the like? a Protestant in receiving the Sacrament; a Papist in the doctrine of the Sacrament? What! do you think there are two heavens? If there be, get you to the other, and place yourselves there; for into this, where I am, you shall never come.'"

This was hearty speech. No one pretended to be ignorant that Laud was meant. People on the back benches stood up to look at him to see how he was taking it, so violent a tirade it was; but he sat unmoved and cold, giving the preacher an impenetrable attention. Against such an adversary nothing could be done. Against ill-feeling and dislike, against public and private affronts, he opposed that magical weapon—indifference. Whenever an opening occurred he took up an unpopular doctrine and preached it—was never violent or discourteous. Like Luther in this respect alone, he enjoyed the feeling of danger. Laud had the key of success, if, as is said, self-possession is the secret of it. When

Buckeridge, by this time President of St. John's, resigned, it became clear that this unpopularity was not going to stand in his way. He had done, without aiming after it, what great characters do —he had impressed those close about him. He was elected President by a clear majority ; but even then the feeling ran so strong that one of the Fellows tore the paper containing the result of the scrutiny out of the bursar's hand, and burnt it. There was an appeal, and Laud was confirmed. Then he set to work to weed out, by fair and polite means, the obnoxious unprogressive Fellows. He got them livings, and eradicated them quietly, till the college was his own. Then he began to procure the election of men after his own heart, " breeding up," as Ascham says of the sister foundation, " so many learned men in that one College of St. John's at one time, as I believe the whole University of Lovaine in many years was not able to afford."

The last person in the world of whom anything is expected nowadays is the master of a college. To be energetic and original is not his forte. To be supreme within the precincts of a noble building, with no defined duties—such a position has a terrible tendency to persuade a man that he has deserved it ; to make him exalt whims and caprices into laws and ordinances. The spirit of Mumbo

Jumbo is apt to prevail in those circles—the spirit of false officialism, the taste for the trappings of authority, the disposition to mistake pomposity for magnificence. None of these things were temptations to Laud. His presidentship gave him a position in the world, and moderate wealth ; it fitted him, in fact, to move one step closer to the centre on which his eyes were fixed. He became at once a learner in another sphere—the sphere of politics, of national movements. He went to Court—the Court of James I.

CHAPTER III.

JAMES the First is one of those figures who would be treated with mere ridicule were he supposed to be the creation of fancy. Such a character would not be tolerated in a fiction—a wilder fusion of incongruous elements than a maker of books would dream of bringing together. Behind a grotesque exterior, padded clothes, and rickety legs, supporting a huge misshapen head, rolling eyes, and a slobbering mouth, lay a profound but unpractical shrewdness, a fund of out-of-the-way knowledge, much humour and power of repartee. "The wisest fool in Christendom," said Henry of Navarre. He was a pedant of the deepest dye : that is to say, he had a German hankering after theory ; he strung theories together from insufficient premisses, and forced subsequent facts into the places he had reserved for them ; he never allowed himself to be corrected by them. On witchcraft, on reprobation, on the Divine right of kings he wrote tractates, in his silly learned fashion. When he visited

Cambridge he made the assembled professors a harangue ; in which, the complimentary addresses said, he outdid them each in his own line. This was not true ; but that a king should attempt such a feat was strangely bewildering. To this he added a fondness for buffoonery and endless chatter, a most despicable cowardice, habitual drunkenness, and possibly other vices. He was ruled by his young favourites, adventurers with pretty faces, whom he fondled and hung upon before the whole Court.

Sir Walter Scott has left, in " The Fortunes of Nigel," perhaps the liveliest and most sympathetic sketch of this undignified monarch, who, weak and wearisome as he was, yet had that affectionate fibre in him which makes him an affectionate memory— rolling about his dusty rooms, plucking a jewel from his hat-buckle in default of money in his purse, and brimming over with quaint Scottish epigram and pungent phrases, striking straight to the heart of the matter with humorous power.

Of course, some of his favourites were mere playthings. The wretched Earl of Rochester, executed for a loathsome poisoning, was not so harmless. But one choice that the king made, surely not wholly by chance, has set its mark on English history.

George Villiers, whose wit, face, and bearing attracted the king's attention, was hurried up the ranks of the peerage, thrust into court offices, made finally the director and dispenser of court favour for the realm. The scenes that are so familiar of the poor monarch in a maudlin fit, crying and kissing " Baby Charles and Steenie," as he loved to call them, are sufficiently degrading. Buckingham, we need make no doubt, found them disgusting too. He was a man too much alive to sensuous and artistic perceptions not to have realized the baseness of the scene ; but he suffered it as a troublesome apprenticeship, through which to climb to a very tangible and unsentimental goal. He was a man with keen ambitions and something of a kingly soul. Disconnect Buckingham from his first adventures, and the means by which he rose, and he appears as a man with much greatness about him. He was strong enough and popular enough, at any rate, to secure the passionate love of his foster-brother and future king. Charles was evidently never in the least jealous of his position ; and at Court, and with the country at large, he maintained his position. There were occasional fits of hostility—one definite attack upon him ; but, considering his origin, it is wonderful that there were no more. He had some of the generous qualities of greatness—a unique devotion to his friends was among them. In Laud's connection with him it is noticeable, I think, that Buckingham's manner, at first businesslike, gradually melts into something warm and personal. Not so Laud. The prayers, " Pro Duce Buckinghamiæ," in his devotions for daily use, and the prayer at the Duke's death, are not edifying or satisfactory compositions. They reflect little genuine personal affection, and a good deal of worldly anxiety. I should be glad to strike them out from my impressions of Laud. What can be made of this sentence? " Continue him a true-hearted friend to me, Thy poor servant, whom Thou hast honoured in his eyes." That is not a noble sentiment for a man to utter secretly, in the presence of God, about his friend. Whether or no Laud loved him—and this is hardly credible—it is certain he owed everything to him. There is no reasonable doubt that the motive which induced Charles to take Laud as his supreme adviser on the duke's death, was the fact that Laud was known to possess Buckingham's confidence, to have been much with him—in fact, his confessor. Laud had owed his original episcopal promotion to Buckingham ; but the seal of his greatness was set by Buckingham's death, and the relation in which he had stood to him when alive.

Poor Buckingham ! the heart goes out after
him. Filled with strange presentiments, he went
heavily down to Portsmouth to die by so unfore-
seen a death ; and the news of his fate, received
by the king with a passion of tears, was the signal
for the little cold far-sighted figure, never unrea-
sonably swayed by any romance or personal bias,
save once, to step into his place and move
onwards in the same line—that line which was so
enigmatic, by being at once imaginative and hard.

This stage of Laud's life is a quiet one—he made
no great parade. It was a period of silent secret
growth—growth of influence, growth of purpose.
All this time he was accumulating weight ; it cannot
be described as making friends, because Laud's
was a cold nature. The sentiments, the close
relations of human life, were wonderfully aloof from
him. He stood in the priestly relation with several,
but that is by no means always an intimate relation,
because it presupposes the accurate knowledge of
facts and thoughts which it would be death to
intimacy to know. In Confession the soul that
seeks for guidance speaks to his confessor as he
would to God, and human beings cannot speak to
one another as they would to God ; there is a kind
of confidence that love ignores.

Only once did this wary self-contained career

halt ; only once did he make a false step. " Dec.
26, 1605, Dies erat Jovis et Festum S^{ti}. Stephani,"
says the Diary, " My cross about the Earl of
Devon's marriage."

Charles Blount, who became Lord Mountjoy
on the death of his elder brother, and afterwards
created Earl of Devonshire, was a soldier of some
repute. He put down the rebellion of the Earl
Tir-owen in Ireland, at the battle of Kinsale, and
in reward for his services was advanced to be Lord
Deputy of that kingdom by James I.

When a younger son, without prospects, he had
set his affections on the Lady Penelope Devereux,
daughter of the Earl of Essex, a most sweet and
attractive maiden, if we can trust contemporaries.
Their troth was plighted, but her friends would
have none of him, and married her out of hand
to an austere uncourtly gentleman, Lord Rich,
who behaved, if not cruelly, at least with great
roughness towards her. Of such romances, where
lover and wife are both weak and passionate, there
can be but one melancholy ending—a sonnet in
the " Arcadia " records the circumstance.

Lord and Lady Rich were divorced. She had
already borne several children—to Mountjoy, it
was known ; for there was no attempt at disguise
throughout.

D

Laud had been made Mountjoy's chaplain, living with him at Wanstead in Essex; there, being much worked upon and, it appears, threatened by the earl—for he was now Earl of Devonshire—he broke down, and married the pair, knowing that only the loosest Calvinism gave anything like a hearty assent to such a match, and that the principles that he himself adhered to, most vigorously condemned it; "serving my ambition, and the sins of others," as he sadly says. He was threatened, it seems certain, with loss of court favour if he refused; and it is not improbable that he had a great friendship for the earl, if not for his lady. It was to temptation of power that he succumbed: the result was precisely the opposite of what he had expected. James, in his capacity as ecclesiastical lawyer, was so angry with the earl that he had to write an apology, and died of "the spleen," that is to say disappointment, within a year. He very nearly involved his chaplain in the disgrace, and it is not improbable that Laud's long waiting for advancement was connected with this false step.

The day was ever after a day of solemn observation and humiliation for him. Four years after there was another mysterious and similar event on the same day—"E.M. Die lunæ, 1609"—some strange sin of which we have lost the secret. "Lapidatus non pro sed a peccato" — "Stoned (like the martyr whose day it was), not *for* but *by* my sin," he writes of it, making the enigma deeper than ever. The Latin prayer which stands first among the " Anniversaria," has reference to these two events, and is in a tone of deep, almost abject abasement. He prays that it may not prove a divorcing of his own soul from the spirit.*

I came, the other day, upon the actual petition of Lord Rich for divorce, filed among the Lambeth papers ; and there is also a curious relic, attributed by tradition to the time of Laud, which has undoubtedly reference to the same event.

This is a portrait, rather stiff and Flemish in style, which hangs in the great corridor of the Palace, of a sweet-faced gentle lady, her bunches of auburn hair standing out very strongly against a pale-green background. On the back, in large old letters, are traced the words, " A Countess of Devonshire." It cannot be doubted which.

* In 1621, when Bishop of St. David's elect, by a curious chance he had to preach before the Court at Wanstead, in the very chapel where he had celebrated this fatal marriage ; he preached on the peace of the Church. The following passage occurs in it : " Yet will I do the People right : for tho' many of them are guilty of inexcusable sin, as sacrilege, so too many of us Priests are guilty of other as great sins as sacrilege, for which no doubt we and our possessions lie open to waste : it must needs be so." This was part of his penance ; none of his hearers can have been ignorant of what he meant.

CHAPTER IV.

A WEARY period of waiting ensued.

Laud was so nearly disgusted with court life, that he resolved to quit it, and was only just persuaded to resume it. Dr. Neile, Bishop of Durham, a man of wonderful tact in choosing remarkable men, though without many gifts himself, except that of amiability, became his patron. He gave him chambers in Durham House. At last James began to relent. He made him a Royal Chaplain, and at last gave him the Deanery of Gloucester. Here he fell into a nest of hornets, but routed them. The cathedral church was in a dismal state. He set about a drastic reform ; in fact, he had been sent there as a kind of experiment. James had no pleasure in neglect and carelessness, and Neile suggested to him that the fearless active Laud would be the very man to reform Gloucester.

Up went the altar to the east, and all the subordinates of the church were compelled to bow to it ; the organ was repaired, the dirt and cobwebs cleared away, new and unfamiliar doctrines preached by the little dauntless Dean. He had burst upon the quiet slumbering western city like a thunder-bolt ; the place had drowsed away into a contented Calvinism.

There is nothing like the resistance of a limited place where gossip can rage. Laud was the best-hated man in Gloucester. The Bishop said that he could not possibly enter the church till that Nehushtan (meaning the altar), had been removed to some less offensive place. For eight years this worthy follower of the Prince of Peace heard the bells call to prayer from the palace study, and thought bitterly of the active Dean scraping and posturing in the well-known choir.

This was stirring enough, but there were larger events to come. In 1616 he accompanied the king to Scotland. James, with that unsympathetic clumsiness whose very *naïveté* disarmed offence, told the Scottish divines that he had brought them a theologian to enlighten their minds a little. Had Laud known it, on this occasion was sown that vast unintermitting Scottish hatred of the man that was so great a factor in his fall. Then he was made Bishop of St. David's, " a poor city, God wot," as Heylyn says. He also held *in commendam*

more than one living. His only visit to his Welsh
cure of souls is so humorous, that I cannot refrain
from quoting it. His coach was overturned twice
in the last seven miles before Abergwili, his palace.
There he consecrated a chapel on the Decollation
of St. John, a day that connected itself with several
other important crises of his life. A Mr. Jones
applied for ordination, but on examination he
proved so widely ignorant, especially of Latin, that
" I sent him away," says Laud, "with an exhorta-
tion, not ordained."

But the great event of this time was his friendship with the Duke of Buckingham—a far more
serious politician, as we have said, considering his
meteoric rise, than is generally allowed. The two
men came naturally together. In those days so
much went by favour, that it was necessary to
fascinate or impress the great personages of the
kingdom in order to succeed. Laud impressed
Buckingham. The following entries in the Diary
are significant.

"Jan. 22. My L^d of B. and I in the inner chamber
at York House. Quod Deus est salvator noster
J. C.*

"June 9, Whitsunday. My Lord M. B. was

* I suppose that this refers to some doubts in the duke's mind
as to the Divinity of our Saviour.

pleased to enter upon a near respect to me : the particulars are not for paper.

"June 15. I became C. to my L^d of B., and June 16 being Trin. Sund. he received the Sacr. at Greenwich." "C." is Confessor. After this, there was no possibility of mistaking Laud for anything but an important man.

The early stages of their intimacy are curious. "When the Duke fell sick of an ague in the beginning of May, he was extreme impatient of his fits, till Laud came to visit him : by whom he was so charmed and sweetened, that at first he endured his fits with patience, and thus did so break their heat and violence that at last they left him."

The projected match between Charles and the Infanta began to cause great uneasiness in the country ; and this was increased by the wild journey to Spain of the prince and Buckingham. Laud was one of the few in the secret ; he corresponded with Buckingham throughout, and when it was thought necessary to conciliate the Pope, whom James had definitely and unmistakably been calling Antichrist in a theological treatise, it was Laud who suggested the lines of the apology—that it was all done argumentatively, " as a man might say." This sent Laud's popularity down lower

still : the dread of the Papacy was fast becoming
morbid in England.

Laud's great quarrel with Abbot, now Archbishop, took place at this time. The members of
Convocation had subsidized the king to the extent
of twenty per cent. of their incomes. Laud, who
knew more about the country clergy than any one,
represented to Buckingham that this meant very
serious sacrifices, and a memorandum was drawn up
to be presented to the king. Laud went to consult
Abbot about it, and that jealous secretive man,
thoroughly angry at Laud's growing and his own
waning influence, told him sharply that, by first
going to a lay lord, without ecclesiastical consulta-
tion, he had inflicted such a wound on the Church
as she would never recover. The expression is
absurdly disproportionate to the offence : and
Laud's answer, under its courtesy of manner, shows
an almost irrepressible disgust and irritation. " He
could not conceive," he said, "what fault he had
committed. The matter had to be settled, and he
had gone to the obvious sources." Professional
jealousy was never a vice of Laud's. After that
time the two never met amicably.

Another enemy of Laud's was a prominent man
—Williams, Bishop of Lincoln, Lord Keeper of the
Privy Seal, and Dean of Westminster. Alarmed at

Laud's growing power and his ominous friendship with Buckingham, he formed with Abbot a secret coalition to defeat it. Williams was a clever shifty man of latitudinarian opinions. He intended to conciliate, even to reconcile the two extremes; he succeeded in making enemies of both. Such has always been the fate of Broad schools. Still, Williams was a man of great ability and moderation, and of strong common sense. His letter to the Vicar of Grantham, where the fiercest altar controversy had taken place, is a model of gentle decision. " I shall esteem him the truest Christian that yields first," he wrote. Williams would have been a very dangerous rival to Laud, not, that is, in the personal sense, but as the representative of a different school, equally adverse to the Puritans; but he fell into disgrace at Court, became unpopular with the king, was finally dismissed on a mere quibble, and had to retire to his diocese, where he wrote moderate letters with indifferent success.

It is curious, but there seems no reason to doubt it, that Williams had been one of the keenest advocates of Laud's elevation to the episcopal bench; the following conversation, whether apocryphal or not, is represented by Bishop Hacket as having taken place between Williams and the king on the subject: it contains so much of James's caustic perceptive humour, that it is well worth reading. How Dean Hook came to omit so valuable a contemporary judgment of Laud it is impossible to understand; he alludes to it in a foot-note as being of uncertain authority. It appears to the general reader, perhaps, the most interesting and acute criticism ever passed upon Laud.

Williams was introduced, and began to plead.

"'Well,' said the king, ' I perceive whose attorney you are; Stenny* hath set you on. You have pleaded the man a good Protestant, and I believe it. Neither did that stick in my breast when I stopped his promotion. But was there not a certain lady who forsook her husband, and married a Lord that was her paramour? Who knit that knot? Shall I make a man a Prelate, one of the angels of my Church, who hath a flagrant crime upon him?' 'Sir,' said the Lord Keeper, ' you are a good master; but who will dare serve you if you will not pardon one fault, though of a scandalous size, to him that is heartily penitent for it? I pawn my faith to you that he is heartily penitent; and there is no other blot that hath sullied his good name.' 'You press well,'

* The Duke of Buckingham.

said the king, 'and I hear you with patience.
Neither will I revive a trespass which repentance
hath mortified and buried.   And because I see that
I shall not be rid of you, unless I tell you my
unpublished cogitations, *the plain truth is I keep
Laud back from all place of rule and authority
because I find he hath a restless spirit and cannot
see when matters are well, but loves to toss and
change, and to bring things to a pitch of reformation floating in his own brain*, which may endanger
the steadfastness of that which, God be praised, is
at a good pass.   I speak not at random : he hath
made himself known to me to be such an one.
For when, three years past, I had obtained of the
Assembly of Perth to consent to five articles of
order and decency in a correspondence with this
Church of England, I gave them promise that I
would try their obedience no further anent ecclesiastical affairs.   Yet this man hath pressed me to
invite them to a nearer conjunction with the Liturgy
and Canons of this nation ; but I sent him back
again, with the frivolous draft that he had drawn.
And now your importunity hath compelled me to
shrive myself thus unto you, I think you are at
your furthest, and have no more to say for your
client.'

  "'May it please you, sir,' replied Williams, 'I

will speak but this once. You have convicted your
chaplain of an attempt very audacious and very
unbecoming. My judgment goes quite against his:
yet I submit this to your sacred judgment: that
Dr. Laud is of a great and tractable wit. He did
not well see how he came into this error; but he
will presently see the way to come out of it. Some
diseases, which are very acute, are quickly cured.'

"'And is there no whoe,* but you must carry it?'
said the king. 'Then take him with you, but, by
my soul, you will repent it!' and so went away
in anger, using other words of fierce and ominous
import, too tart to be repeated."

The explanation of this seemingly enthusiastic
advocacy is not creditable to Williams: he was
anxious to retain his Deanery of Westminster.
Had he resigned it, it must have fallen to Laud,
whom he disliked very much, both the man and his
principles; consequently he advised his removal to
St. David's in a way which, to the unprejudiced
reader, will appear strangely disinterested; any
careful student, however, of Williams' life is forced
to conclude that such a course of proceeding was
so unfamiliar to the Lord Keeper as to make the
plain reading of his conduct impossible.

But just at this point a strange and unfore-

* Way.

seen accident occurred. Abbot, hunting at Lord
Zouch's park at Bramshill, in Eversley parish,
had the misfortune to kill a keeper. This in-
voluntary homicide, making him, as it was technically called, "a man of blood," had the effect
of suspending him from many of the duties of his
position. "I wish," wrote the Lord Keeper to
the Duke of Buckingham—"I wish with all my
heart his Majesty would be as merciful as ever
he was in all his life. To add affliction unto the
afflicted (as no doubt he is in mind) is against
the King's nature: to leave a man of blood Primate
and Patriarch of all his churches, is a thing that
sounds very harsh in the old Councils and Canons
of the Church." The case was a difficult one. It
was argued that the Archbishop had no right to be
hunting at all; that he was acting feloniously in so
doing. If this was the case, it turned what was
otherwise little more than a deplorable incident into
a crime; just as a burglar, nowadays, who dislodges
a tile from a house roof may, if it proves fatal to any
one in the street, be tried for murder. This kind of
case, turning on antique precedents and pedantic
pleas, delighted the king; he flung himself into it.
Coke, the great lawyer, saved Abbot: he dragged to
light an immemorial statute that a bishop's *morte*
of hounds was to escheat to the king on his decease,

not to the natural heirs. Ergo, argued Coke, he
may hunt with them when he is alive if they are
to pass to some one else on his death. Abbot,
however, though legally acquitted, was still debarred
from spiritual functions, his powers and official
duties were placed in commission, and he retired
to the melancholy seclusion of the hospital that he
had built at Guildford, whose red brick towers are
the glory of the High Street still.

Besides this, though not, it was said, naturally
a harsh or unfeeling man, he had been particularly
unfortunate in his domestic relations. His only
brother, Robert, was made Bishop of Salisbury
at the age of sixty-five, and shortly afterwards
announced to his friends his intention of marrying
a young lady of his acquaintance. Upon this, in
the double character of injured brother and indig-
nant metropolitan, the Archbishop, who chose to
consider the proceeding a public scandal, wrote his
brother a letter so stern and vindictive in tone,
that the poor man died literally of a broken heart
in a few months—no one even professed to give
any other explanation. Abbot was considerably
shocked at the result of his epistle. His shafts
were seldom harmless.

When the unhappy man returned to Lambeth
he deliberately began a policy, suggested by

suspicious jealousy, which reduced his influence to a cipher ; he never appeared in public, but confined himself to the palace, and let the whole place wear the disguise of a haunt of conspirators : from across the river the tall windows flamed all night ; there were midnight gatherings, secret conclaves, all the more contemptible because they effected nothing. He and his friends were named the Nicodemites, because they came and went by night. It became a mere rendezvous of all disaffected, discontented persons in Church or State. His portrait, handsome, pale, thin-featured, has a very melancholy look, next Laud's brisk work-a-day face.

James died suddenly of an ague at Theobald's. Laud, who happened to be preaching at Whitehall, broke off his sermon when the news came in, hearing the Duke of Buckingham's open lamentations. And Prince Charles was proclaimed. It is an excusable dream to think how differently all might have gone if the generous kindly Prince Henry of Wales had lived to succeed, who had said in boyish enthusiasm that when he was king Charles should be Archbishop. Henry and Charles would have been very different from Charles and Laud.

Laud was in his fifty-second year when the assassination of the Duke of Buckingham, at Ports-

mouth, by a debauched maniac named Felton, out
of private enmity, threw another great chance into
his hands—he became First Minister of the Crown.
He had been Bishop of Bath and Wells for nearly
two years, and now he became Bishop of London.
Charles already, by a fatal instinct, had begun to
select men for his advisers and ministers who were
uncompromising advocates of the autocracy of the
Crown.   Laud was one of these, Strafford another.
It is necessary to remember that the common un-
judging estimate of Charles as a man with elements
of weakness and sentimentality in his composition
is utterly unfounded.   He was tenacious and stubborn, intensely irritated at the smallest show of disobedience, profoundly indifferent to public opinion,
and entirely under the domination of one idea—the
prerogative of monarchy.   Such a character was sure
to attract to itself characters working on similar lines
—and politics and religion shared the field of life
in those days.   There did not then exist that large
and growing class who are indifferent to both.   So
Laud and Strafford, with their magnificent indifference to opinion, their absolute determination to
be obeyed, their strong illogical minds, accepting
and never questioning facts, taking the Royal
Supremacy for granted, and Episcopacy as an
institution dear to God, necessarily became his

chosen ministers. It was a triumvirate working single-handed against the whole force of a nation —a triumvirate, it is true, with certain mechanical and traditional advantages. But in the face of the great explosion of democracy the triumvirate was blown away.

CHAPTER V.

ANY one who visited the Vandyck exhibition at the
end of 1886, could not have failed, I believe, to be
struck with the two portraits of Strafford.   In the
first place, by reason of their extreme dissimilarity.
Without the catalogue none but a very critical eye
would have divined that they were portraits of the
same person.   One was painted in his earlier days,
when he was nothing more than an energetic, public-
spirited Yorkshire squire ; the other, on which consequently the interest centres, was after public and
private troubles, passionate loyalty, and a despotic
authority had set their mark upon the face.   The
least imaginative could not have passed the latter
portrait by with indifference, even if ignorant of the
subject.   There is a violence and a vehemence in
the face, a sullen directness which arrests the attention.   No engraving has ever done justice to this.
The iron cuirass out of which the stalwart head
springs seems to be a natural adjunct for such a

face ; the great lowering lines on the brow, the converging eyes, the heavy jaw, all speak of a temper born to rule and encouraged by fortune to do so.   It has not often fallen to the lot of an English citizen to wield so despotic a power as Strafford was enabled to exercise.

Of all the figures of the Caroline court, this man was Laud's chosen friend.   " It is in sadness," writes Strafford to the Archbishop, " that I have wondered many times to observe how universally you and I agree in our judgment of persons, as most commonly we have done ever since I had the honour to be known to you."   They were both of them absolutely possessed by devotion to the cause of royal prerogative.   It was the unconscious action of this blind triumvirate, Charles and his two uncompromising servants, that broke open the clouds of rebellion and drew the tempest down which engulfed them first.

Let us have a little picture of Thomas Wentworth, Earl of Strafford, in our minds, to give us the idea of the qualities which Laud worshipped, his ideal of the public servant, to which his cold nature came spontaneously out in friendship— making them into that pair who were, as Hamilton said, the one too great to fear, and the other too bold to fly.

He was a Yorkshire man. He succeeded to a baronetcy and a very plentiful estate when quite a young man ; he had one of the best incomes in the kingdom. When he first came up to London, after a thorough quiet self-education at St. John's, Cambridge, and abroad, he attracted much attention by a kind of undefinable atmosphere of power that hung about him, and a magnificent insolence in his demeanour. "Dammy," Lord Powis said when it was pointed out that he was of blood royal, "if he ever comes to be king of England, I will turn rebel." He married a daughter of the Earl of Cumberland, and then sat down apparently to do nothing. He watched life ; he made some peaceful friends, such as Sir H. Wotton, Provost of Eton, whose gentle cloistered letters read very peacefully in his agitated correspondence ; he attended the Star Chamber ; he read and wrote ; and down at Wentworth-Wodehouse, his waste park, he contracted the passionate love for sport and country life that comes out in such natural sighs in the letters he wrote when worn with disease and state troubles, as lord of that unruly isle. His taste in reading was curious. Donne was his favourite author, an uneasy metaphysical poet. Laud laughs at this in one of his letters ; he hints that if Strafford wishes to learn the secret of life, the true valuation of mortality, let him read a chapter in Ecclesiastes—better than all the anagrams of Dr. Donne, " or even," he adds ironically, " the designs of Van Dike," Strafford's favourite painter.

Strafford, for we will call him by his later well-known title, was a man of stormy pride. " I have hated," he said, " to borrow my being from any man." Buckingham was at this time the dispenser of all court patronage, so supreme that it was well known that there was no way to power but through him. Laud had availed himself of this ; it did not revolt Laud to take his hand and be assisted up. But it revolted Strafford. There was some obscure quarrel between the two ; letters passed, hinting on Buckingham's side that a genial submission would help him : Strafford, however, utterly disdained to respond.

A little gentle pressure was tried. Strafford was pricked for sheriff, which disqualified him for parliament ; and he was dismissed from the office of Custos Rotulorum for Yorkshire, the letter from Buckingham announcing it being brought to him in court when he was sitting as justice of the peace in the petty sessions. This drew from him his first public utterance—a passionate dignified appeal to his public services ; a grave avowal of his conscientious purpose ; and a significant hint, which shows that both he and his audience knew only too plainly that he was being sacrificed to a private feud.

It is another instance of the lack of instinctive perception in Charles and his advisers that the most wildly loyal man in all his dominions—and they were becoming a rare species—should have been so deliberately discouraged at the outset. Had not loyalty been a real devouring and consuming passion in Strafford, this would have killed it.

It was followed by a demand for money, under the Great Seal, on some obscure legal precedent : this was refused, and Strafford was actually imprisoned in the Marshalsea.

When he came out he found himself in strange company—so strange, that it has led some writers to believe that Strafford was a Radical turned Royalist; with Pym and Prynne he joined in the ferocious assault on Buckingham, on the occasion on which Laud suggested the lines of his apology before the House. This was the turning-point. It was at last realized by Charles what a capacity for devotion was in the man ; he was no longer dallied with, but received with open arms and splendid honours. He was made a viscount, and Lord President of the North — a kind of ex-

aggerated lord lieutenancy, a reward enough to
gratify the most ambitious courtier. No wonder
that he was called a turncoat; no wonder that
he was treated as a mere venal slave of pomp and
power; no wonder that, after an angry conference
with Pym, they parted with the following prophetic
words echoing in Strafford's ears : "You are going
to leave us, my lord ; but I will never leave you
while your head is on your shoulders."

Before long, the Lord Deputyship of Ireland fell
vacant, and Strafford went naturally thither. In
1633 he was settled at Dublin. Then began that
kind of rule to which it is impossible to give an
unqualified approval, but the narrative of which
gives the same sort of pleasure to the reader as the
account of a prize-fight where the little dogged man
floors his gigantic opponent. Strafford was indomitable throughout ; he never let there be any
mistake about what he meant to do : he had come
over to Ireland to rule the country, and rule it he
would. " Where I found," he said, "a Crown, a
Church, a people spoiled, I could not imagine to
redeem them from under the pressure with gentle
looks ; it would cost warmer water than so."

The Irish Council was an insolent patronizing
body, who looked upon their own permanence and
local influence as far more weighty than the

apparent precedence of an alien head.   Strafford
let them find out their mistake.   He obtained from
the king several royal privileges : he forced the
Council to uncover in his presence, while he sat
with his hat on ; he forbade any conversation at the
Board—if any one wished to speak, he must speak
to the Deputy ; he kept them hours waiting till he
was at leisure, to destroy their false sense of importance.   He gave them what he called " round
answers."   When they spoke of sending a petition
to the king, he informed them that he was the
mouth who came to answer for them all.   He
introduced his two oldest friends, Radcliffe and
Wandesford, to the Board, and made them Councillors.   He reformed the etiquette of Dublin Castle,
which had apparently sunk low.   Great noblemen had been accustomed to walk in and out
of the presence for interviews without asking
leave.   Strafford denied himself to them and
kept them waiting too.   Drinking toasts had become a regular part of the Deputy's daily public
dinner.   " Deep drinking is too universal a fault
in Ireland to-day," said Strafford ; " there shall be
no toast drunk but the king."

All this is the more forcible from the undoubted
fact that it did not proceed from a man who was
either pompous or authoritative in ordinary life ;

it was a deliberate policy directed to a definite end. At Wentworth-Wodehouse, Strafford hunted and shot all day, splashed about in marshes after wild duck, stalked deer, and hawked. In the evening he told stories over a pipe of tobacco. No formalism there ; it was not the nature of the man.

His creation of the Irish parliament is a very notable instance of this. A parliament was Charles's aversion ; he did his best to discourage the step. " No," said Strafford ; " the king must have money. He can take it, it is true, but it is better voted— the parliament shall vote it." He was not afraid of parliaments. He dragged to light the obsolete Poyning's Act, which limited the discussions of the parliament to such subjects as the Deputy and Council should originate. So, with much pomp and antique ceremonial, a parliament was called. Peers, in order of degree, walked in procession, escorting the Deputy in royal state. And he made them a tremendous speech, at which they sat aghast and open-mouthed. " England was giving subsidies," this was the substance of it, " for the king's purposes, which were, as it happened, those of national defence. Ireland must not hope to escape. Vote money for the king, without clogs or conditions." It was " the king " throughout. Six subsidies, amounting to £180,000,

a larger sum than Ireland had ever voted, or than
Strafford had conceived that she would vote, were
eventually declared.   It had been one man against
a nation, one man of rude fiery vehemence, who
knew his own mind thoroughly : and he conquered,
as such men will.

Alas ! the physical constitution was not equal
to this iron soul.   "Well, spoken it is, good or bad,"
wrote Strafford to Laud about this very speech,
" I cannot tell whether ; but whatever it was, I
spake it not betwixt my teeth, but so loud and
heartily that I protest it unto you that I was faint
withal at the time, and the worse for it two or three
days after."   And all through the Irish letters,
though there is no complaint, yet the ill health is
a constant excuse for business which has been
necessarily set aside.   The stone, agonizing attacks
of gout, agues, fainting-fits broke and tortured the
body, but never tamed the indomitable mind.

Before Strafford set out for Ireland, Laud, then
Bishop of London, had a long and secret interview
with him at Fulham.   They had been gradually
drawn together, not by affectionate natures—for
though Strafford's was ardent and impulsive,
Laud's was undeniably cold—but by the enthusiasm
of a common purpose, and by what gives perhaps
a still stronger footing for intimacy—a *common*

method. If two men have to work together the surest recipe for disintegrating their friendship is that their methods of work should jar; slovenliness and the want of pigeon-holing and docketing habits have marred more intimacies than gentleness and common admiration of high things have cemented. Jean Paul has shown us how love is slain, not so much by variance of temperament and aim, as by unseasonable bonnets and an untimely besom. Laud and Strafford worked on identical lines. They had both a fondness for detail that was perhaps extravagant: prosperity and increase expressed themselves for both in material outlines. If Ireland was at peace with itself it should have a flourishing fabric trade, and the Customs should make a handsome return to the king; if the Church was prospering, in Laud's view it should have its altars in the right places, the fabrics should be in repair, the service should be worthy of its Divine origin and end. And Strafford, too, beside the attraction which Laud's similarity of character had for him, found a reverential relief in acting with a great spiritual superior. Closely connected with the sacredness of royal power, was the inherent royalty of sacred persons. The Church came next to the king with Strafford, and they were indissolubly connected.

What was settled at this conclave we do not
exactly know, but we can make a very fair guess.
There were certain rampant abuses of patronage,
and spoliation of the Church, in Ireland ; this had
all to be set to rights. This was the detail, the
individual issue on which they came to terms ; then
Laud probably opened out his general policy, and
received assurances from Strafford of his loyalty
to the same cause. It is one of those memorable
conjunctions of which one thinks with wonder :
the two eager men—Laud fresh and plump, with
sparkling eyes, pacing up and down as was his
wont ; Strafford sitting with his chin upon his hand,
partly sunk down in a chair, as he was used to sit,
feeling perhaps the first lassitude of ill health.
And the keen scheming, on so noble, so hope-
less, so mistaken a line, gives the occasion a pathos
which is infinitely increased by the strange doom
that overshadowed both, and of which, in their
abundance of life and energy and importance, they
so little dreamed. There is no recorded instance
of their meeting again, or seeing each other's faces
till they met in the Tower in the last sad act of the
drama.

At all events, they then or afterwards invented
a mysterious cipher, embracing their policy : some
of this is clear and unmistakable ; some has, I

think, never been interpreted. THOROUGH is too well known to require much elucidation. That was to be their watchword. From the highest down to the lowest all were to serve the king in singleness of heart. There were to be no back thoughts. All who held office under the king, who were his chosen ministers of government, were to be ever thus.

"Them that go thorough for our master's service."

"All able, and all hearty, and all running one way, and none caring for any ends so the king be served," is Laud's expression of the ideal Government (October 14, 1633).

The Lady Mora or Delay, to whom constant allusion is made, seems to embody the opposite principle, especially as exemplified in the Home Council. There Laud could not quite get his way. There were potent lords and councillors, such as Weston and Cottington, who worked on private motives, and still were influential with the king. That could not be amended; but Ireland was a virgin block, to be carved to whatever Strafford would.

On one occasion (July 3, 1634), Laud speaks of "his cipher being packed up for Croydon, else he would tell him how little rest he was likely to have . . . and somewhat else."

But as far as we are concerned his cipher is packed up for many passages. I feel certain, after studying the letters, that many passages of seeming unimportance, where the two seem to be indulging in mere personal banter, contain secrets of State. I believe there is much to be extracted yet from the letters if only one could hold the key.

I venture to quote one of the many unintelligible passages. Can anything be made of it?

"In the next place you begin to be merry with your Heifer, and I wonder you have so little pity as not to let it rest when I have plowed with it. By St. Dunstan (if it were not for swearing), I see you guess unhappily that your friends can tell how to be merry as well as serious together, and you shall not need to intreat us to continue it, for we have no other purpose, only I am in ill case by it. For your Spaniard, and the gravity which he learnt there, while he went to buy Pigeons, has tempted my old friend the Secretary from me, and he is become his man."

These passages have no apparent allusion to anything that precedes or follows them ; they seem to be perfectly isolated : and it must be concluded that they are a cipher of some kind. Again, there is an expression, "Peccatum ex te, Israel," which stood for some line of action, or the result of some policy. I find it in places where its natural rendering can have no sort of application.

The correspondence of Strafford occupies two folio volumes. They consist of letters which he received or wrote from the beginning of his public life. The collection would be an interesting one, as containing the epistolary expression of the thoughts and politics of all the leading men of the day. And it is agreeably diversified by long scandalous chronicles, containing all the main gossip of the fashionable world, from Mr. Garrard, the master of the Charterhouse, who was apparently pledged to keep Strafford *au fait* with all the news of the town.

There are about twenty of Laud's letters in the collection—at first rather formal, but unbending often enough into a species of frigid fun, which, by its antique form and crabbed range, has forfeited all the humour it can have ever possessed, but by no means the interest. It shows the kind of clumsy word-juggling that passed for wit of a grave statesmanlike kind among the Caroline men of affairs.

The metaphor that is perhaps commonest throughout the letters is that of "vomiting" and "purging" the lay appropriations of Church property. The grasping Churchmen themselves that then infested Ireland pass under the names of Church Cormorants, Ravens, and other opprobrious titles; they are to be trounced, and made to disgorge what they have swallowed. And when we compare this with the fact that property worth £30,000 a year was actually refunded to the Church in Ireland under Strafford's administration, we feel that the purging was at once drastic and effectual.

The Bishops had set the example. They had done unheard-of things. They sold the leases of woods and wastes for several lives. In one place a Bishop had leased the palace to his son for fifty years. Six preferments was a small number for an important dignitary to hold. Strafford, on the spot, and Laud beckoning across the Channel, set these quiet roosters cackling. Such a stirring up of dust there was, such a flutter; but, with those determined men at work, no complaints, only doleful entreaties and melancholy submission. The Archbishop of Armagh has no altar even in his chapel. " No bowing there, I warrant," says Strafford. " Poor Beagle!" he says of himself; with his nose to the ground he patiently tracked these abuses out.

Among these cares the two careful men have time to exchange presents and hatch little plans and private ventures. The Archbishop wants a gown of furs; he would like marten-skins (the pine-marten, then a familiar denizen of Ireland). Dried fish for the Lenten table at Croydon comes from the Deputy, and an apology for the scanty supply of furs. Laud suggests elaborate pisciculture of salmon and trout, unless—which is, perhaps, more probable—this is merely another cipher. I give the reference (October 20, 1634). Strafford tells him of the wooden hunting-lodge he is building down at Wicklow, or his sport at "Cosha, the Park of Parks," as he dates his letters, "the finest moun-tain desolate place I ever saw." "You think," says Laud, "to stop my mouth with some of your hung beef out of Yorkshire; which, to your skill and commendation be it spoken, was the worst I ever tasted, and as hard as the very horn the old Runt wore when she lived. But I wonder you do not think of powdering or drying some of your Irish venison, and send that over to bray too. Well, there's enough of this stuff!"

Strafford evidently thinks that Laud is finding fault with his love of sport; for by this time the correspondence has become very outspoken and easy; so he ridicules delicately Laud's suggestions about pisciculture, and gives some clear reasons. "Perchance you think now," he says, "I learn

F

nothing going up yonder amongst them into the Forests and Rocks."

Or Laud's superstitious mind comes out. A certain mad lady, the Dame Eleanor Davies, whose story we shall allude to more in detail elsewhere, prophesied Laud's death on the 5th of November. "I make no matter of it," he says. But why does he allude to it, even though half-laughingly, in his next three letters? And Strafford thinks it worth while to encourage him.

They are business-like letters for the most part. Laud's weariness creeps in in little natural sentences. He closes one letter abruptly; "he can keep his eyes open no longer; it is so late." He is evidently overrun with work. In one letter Strafford tells Laud with great exactness—he evidently means it to be repeated—his exact increase of fortune since he entered the king's service. There had evidently been calumnious statements made. He has laid away £13,000 in nine years. Considering that his private fortune was £6000 a year, equal to perhaps £40,000 now, it is a wonderful proof of his incorruptibility and absence of self-interest. In similar situations many people had raised themselves to the fortune and condition of peers. In one letter the intimacy has even gone so far that Laud delicately chides him for marry-

ing his third wife. However, he says he is sure
he has had good reason ; deploring, with a half-
humorous pathos, the wife—Official Drudgery—to
whom he himself is now so hopelessly mated.

Every now and then there are some sweet human
touches. " In good earnest," writes Strafford from
Dublin Castle, " I should wax exceeding melancholy
were it not for two little girls that come now and
then to play with me."

His letters to the Countess of Clare about his
children are simply affectionate. He writes from
Fairwood, his own Irish estate, just before he
crossed to Anglesea at the beginning of the Rebellion, a long letter all about his darlings. " Nan,
they tell me, danceth prettily. Arabella is a small
practitioner that way also, and they are both very
apt to learn that or anything that they are taught.
Their brother is just now sitting at my elbow, in
good health, God be praised."

And so the correspondence drops ; and the friends
meet no more till the Tower unites them, and even
then they are not permitted to have speech of one
another.

The word "devoted" is used of Laud's friendships. Hook uses it of the relation on both sides.
This, I cannot help feeling, was a mistake ; a man
without wife or child is allowed a little of passion

in his friendships ; but passion was not in Laud's vocabulary. It is true he was bitterly moved, he fell to the ground "in animi deliquio" when he spoke the words of blessing. But there is little of the David and Jonathan about it : there is no hungering for the personal relation, of individual man for individual man, that is the essence of all friendship ; there is an elated consciousness of the same solemn mission, a common attachment to a great intermediate cause. But the friendship is, so to speak, common, not mutual ; it was not followed for itself, but sprang from circumstances, and kept circumstances in view all along. Such direct pleasure as the intimacy afforded was by the way, πάρεργον, not followed for itself. They were friends because they were patriots. Human nature cannot help wishing that they had been patriots because they were friends.

CHAPTER VI.

IT will here be as well to give a brief account of some of the circumstances that brought Laud into extreme odium with the Puritan and democratic party. " Like a busic and an angry waspe, his sting is in the tail of everything," they said. His determined enmity to popular liberty as opposed to autocratic government may be said broadly to have been the cause of his downfall. I do not suppose that it was, even at the time, summed up in such words : "Liberty," "the rights of the masses," " the will of the people" were not party cries then ; but public opinion expressed itself in its extreme readiness to adopt any accusation, probable or possible, against him. In most minds this consisted in identifying him with the Papal tyranny, making him an ardent though secret advocate in the cause of reconciling the two Churches.

This will be illustrated by the three episodes which I have selected to indicate the line he adopted, and the light in which it was viewed by his opponents,—his connection with the queen, the case of Richard Montague, and his censorship of the press.

It is clear that the queen obtained a gradual ascendency over Charles, an ascendency which she did not at first possess ; and nothing in Laud's court life incurred such suspicion in the country as his intimate connection with her Majesty. It must be looked upon as a most unfortunate event that Charles should have chosen at that juncture a Roman Catholic wife, and that she should have been of that peculiarly un-English type that Henrietta Maria represented. But it was merely another stroke from that persistent ill fortune which pursued Charles from first to last.

She was a high-spirited child, of quick and generous emotions and passionate impulses ; romantically interested in the young king at first, and blankly disappointed when she found he was not all she had imagined. But her freaks and fancies, her pettishness and her pathos, and, most of all, her religion, merely struck the hard gloomy Roundheads of the time with a sense of painful disgust. She chose, too, with fatal precision, the very prejudices at that time so dear to the Puritans to insult and mock at.

At Titchfield, when, against her wishes, the Protestant service was continued in the house in the king's absence, she disturbed the preacher by planning a malevolent laughing expedition into the room with her train of chattering maidens, and sweeping through, to the consternation of the assembled servants and the preacher staring over his cushions.

Again, what is more touching than her visit to Tyburn, in the course of a ramble, and the natural tears she shed in the sight of a gaping crowd at the thoughts of the martyrs who had there laid down their lives for the faith so dear to herself, and yet. so hopelessly perished out of the land ? It was this last performance that made Charles, for once in his life, ungentle. He locked her into the private apartments at Whitehall, and told her brutally that he had issued orders for the immediate banishment of all her ladies and attendants back to France. The poor young queen, passionately attached as she was to all that recalled her happier childhood and the sunny land she had left, hearing voices below, dashed her hand through the window-pane to call for help, and was actually dragged away by her irritated husband, with bleeding fingers. And what can be sadder or more human than Charles's own account of a bitter interview that took place one night between them, after they were in bed, about her jointure? "Take your lands to yourself," said the queen. "If I have no power to put whom I will into those places, I will have neither lands nor houses of you. Give me what you think fit by way of pension."

"Remember," said Charles, having recourse to his authoritative manner,—"remember to whom you speak. You ought not to use me so." At this the poor young queen broke down and cried, saying she was utterly miserable. She had no power. Business that she took an interest in fared worse for her recommendation.. She was not of that base quality to be used so ill. At last Charles insisted upon being heard. "I made her end that discourse," he says.

Rough measure though it was to send away her friends, it had its desired effect. She learnt to lean on and to love her husband, and thus gained that influence over him which those who seem to lean on a stubborn nature will always gain. Charles began to show signs of making dangerous concessions. It is true he interfered when she took the Prince Charles to Mass, but he began to make great allowances for her religion.

About this time an emissary of the Pope's,

Panjani by name, visited England, with the intention of getting better terms, if possible, for the English Catholics through the intervention of the queen. He had long conferences with Windebank and Cottington, Secretaries of State. The latter even went so far as to raise his hat whenever the Pope's name was mentioned. Panjani even distributed artificial flowers and sacred pictures among the gentlemen of the Court. He thus felt he had prepared a real basis of operations; that he had got a hold, though a flimsy one, upon the Court. He even had a talk with Bishop Montague, the old controversialist, who suggested several grounds of concession upon which the two Churches might meet. But every one felt that this was merely playing over the surface. In the background of all these leisurely conversations there lurked the hard-headed clear-sighted personality of the Archbishop. There was nothing misty about him. Montague told Panjani that he had been talking to him, but that Laud was very "timid and circumspect." The conversation languished after that.

Laud was approached through the queen. On August 30, 1634, he enters in his Diary that the queen sent for him to Oatlands, and gave him thanks for a business which she had trusted him withal, promising him to be his friend, and that he should have immediate access to her when he had occasion. Again, on May 18, 1635, he writes that he brought his account to the queen on Whit-Sunday, and received from her an assurance of all that was desired by him.

It was in the winter between these dates that Panjani came to London, and it is impossible not to connect the entries with that event. Panjani's first attempt was to get leave from Charles to have a Catholic Bishop in England, nominated by the king, and acting under such limitations as the king should impose ; but this certainly met with no countenance from Laud, and the king was obliged to discourage it. Panjani's mission came to nothing, except to discredit Laud still more in the eyes of the extreme party.

They believed him guilty of a deliberate attempt to foist the Pope on England. Libellous squibs and anagrams fell fast and furious. There are several of them bound up in the Lambeth papers, annotated and dated with his own hand. The letters of his name, WILLLAM LAUDE, furnished the scurrilous with the most popular of all—WELL, I AM A DIVEL. A paper was dropped at the south gate of St. Paul's, declaring that the devil had let that house to him for the saying of Mass and other abominations. Another was fastened to the north gate, saying that the Church of England was like a candle in a snuff, going out in a stench. These are contemptible details, but they pleased the taste of the times, and serve to show which way the tide of popular feeling was running.

We must now return to an event which took place towards the end of James's reign.

Richard Montague, B.D., Chaplain in Ordinary to the King, who has been mentioned above, was Fellow of Eton College, Canon of Windsor, and Rector of Stanford-Rivers, in Essex. Near this village stood a lonely grange in retired fields, long deserted, which was at last taken by a mysterious tenant, who never set foot outside its walls by day, but came and went by night. Before long it was found that there were several tenants, and it soon transpired that it was the haunt of a number of Jesuits, actively engaged in proselytizing in the neighbouring country.

Montague, who was a man of an active and argumentative mind, with strong High-Church opinions, wishing to preserve his own parish from these night-spirits, managed to communicate with them. He proposed a trial of skill. If they could logically convince him, he would at once join them.

In a few days a little pamphlet, closely written,

was dropped in the night into his study. It was entitled, "A New Gag for an Old Gospel," and contained a confutation out of the English Bible of the Protestant position,—and a note was attached, begging that he would answer it in detail.

On perusing the pamphlet, he found that it contained a refutation, not of the orthodox Protestant position, but of a heterogeneous mass of Calvinistic fancies, representing, perhaps, the extreme poles of Puritan opinion, but thoroughly heterodox in tone.

Montague wrote a careful reply, called the "Gagger," which was received with a storm of abuse and recrimination from the Calvinists. It caused the same sort of sensation that the publication of "Essays and Reviews" caused in modern days. It revealed to the Puritans generally how much opinion there was among the higher dignitaries of the Church that lay in close proximity to the doctrines of the Church of Rome ; and the Church of Rome was for them almost identical with the kingdom of Satan. The Pope himself was Antichrist—the king had said so.

But James had been broadening his views since he had known the English theologians. He held out a helping hand to Montague, and advised him to publish a little book refuting the chief of the accusations made against him. This book shortly appeared, with the title of " Appello Cæsarem."

At this point the king died, somewhat unseasonably, and, in the confusion that ensued, what with Prince Charles's accession and his marriage, it might have been hoped that Montague would escape. But the Puritans had not forgotten.

He was cited before the House of Commons, and condemned to a fine of £2000 and imprisonment. Charles acted with characteristic promptitude and spirit. He gave the House to understand that Montague was one of his chaplains, and that he did not like this high-handed method of procedure. But the Commons were stubborn. They referred the matter to the Committee of Religion then sitting, by whom Montague was solemnly condemned as having attempted a reconciliation of the English Church with Popery. The fine was not rescinded.

Just at this moment the see of Chichester fell vacant, and, by Laud's advice, Montague was appointed. He was now out of the reach of the Commons. He took his seat as a peer, passing through their midst. With him went Dr. Mainwaring, the new Bishop of St. David's, who had fallen similarly under the displeasure of the Lower House.

Of course the Commons—hard godly Puritans, stern and serious—were profoundly angry. It was a victory which Laud and his supporters keenly enjoyed—to carry away the booty unharmed from out of the very jaws of the enemy. Heylyn makes very merry over it. He evidently feels that it was a well-merited lesson ; that the House was taking upon itself functions that lay quite outside its range. They were there, he believes, to vote subsidies, not to hold proceedings in controversial theology. He has a very amusing passage, where he contends that they caught the habit, like an epidemic, from a session held in the Divinity School at Oxford. He imagines it must have turned their heads. The House of Commons enthroned in a Divinity School ! The Speaker in a Regius Professor's chair ! A vision, he insists, must have flashed across them of supremacy, not only in politics, but in theology. And he ends with a most humorous comparison to Vibius Rufus, who, having married Cicero's widow and bought Cæsar's chair, felt himself in a fair way to acquire the eloquence of one and the power of the other.

In 1637 a measure of Laud's was passed in the Star Chamber which, perhaps, aroused a wider and more bitter hostility against him than any other of his unpopular enactments. It was a severe curtailment of the liberty of the press. The decree was a singularly stringent one. It limited the number of printers, and it forbade the printing or reprinting of any book without a licence from the Archbishop of Canterbury, the Bishop of London, or the Chancellors of Oxford and Cambridge. Laud held two of these dignities himself, and his friend and *protégé*, the gentle and submissive Juxon, was Bishop of London.

Thus the committee was a small one, and had a very decided bias. It was a grievous mistake for a man to make : but, on the other hand, it was a very excusable one ; for a man accustomed to have his way, and determined to have his way, and devoid of the smallest intention of either interpreting or humouring the prejudices or wishes of the people, profoundly convinced that his duty was to *govern* them, it was a natural mistake—so natural, indeed, that it is impossible to conceive his acting otherwise.

The little pocket Bible, with foot-notes — the Genevan edition—was one of the first publications suppressed. Two whole editions were seized at the Hague. They were cheap, convenient, well-printed little books, and they were correct—while in the last English editions of the Bible and Prayer Book over a thousand errors had been detected ; for instance in the Commandments in Exodus, the seventh stood as " Thou shalt commit adultery." For no step has the Archbishop incurred more odium. It has been called a piece of true prelatical oppression. He is even supposed to have deliberately set his face against the circulation of the Word of God.

But if we examine the character of this book, we are compelled to decide that, in the first place, Laud could not have done otherwise, and, in the second place, that it was a vile and fanatical work.

The notes were abominable ; so wild are they, that they are little short of ludicrous to us now. They laid down the principles that kings might be disobeyed and assassinated if they were idolaters ; that promises were not binding if upon examination they proved to run counter to the gospel ; that the Presbytery was of Divine importance; adding, as a corollary established beyond the possibility of doubt, in so many words, that Archbishops, Bishops, and all holders of academical degrees were the locusts of the Apocalypse that came up out of the pit.

In his trial the Archbishop maintained that he was not in the least sorry for having thus acted, and that if he had the power he would do so again ; and all rational people will be of his mind.

Whether he exerted his prerogative wisely in the

case of other books may be doubted. Probably much was suppressed that would have condemned itself; and more harm was done by the keeping under of seditious nonsense than would ever have been caused by its appearance.

CHAPTER VIII.

LAUD had evidently experienced that deep attraction to cloistered contemplative life that thoughtful men whose lines are cast in busy places are apt to feel. He sighed, in the whirl and rush of official work, for rest and study, peace and prayer. He would not have been human if he had not. Just as the wistful eremite looks back, in moments of reaction, half-heartedly, to all the stir and freshness he has left, which reach him so faintly through the gratings of his retreat ;—so Laud sighed for retirement, well knowing that he would make no sacrifices to win it, and that he would be unhappy under it, were it forced by fate upon him.

And so he sought out devotional men and made much of them. He promoted Cosin and Jeremy Taylor. He came across the path of George Herbert at the most critical moment of his life. Herbert was at Wilton, with his cousin the Earl of Pembroke, in an undecided mood, feeling drawn to the religious life, but not assured of his call. Let us recall the circumstances of the dilemma; for few decisions have ever conferred so much attractiveness upon the Church as the decision which revealed to Herbert his true vocation.

George Herbert was the younger brother of the famous rationalist—Deist, as they called him then, —Lord Herbert of Cherbury. He belonged to one of the highest and most famous families of the kingdom, had independent means, and delicate student's tastes, and a strong perception of the beauty of religion. The only faults his affectionate tutor found in him were his love of dainty dress, and his aloofness from any companionship which had anything low or unrefined about it. This beautiful figure grew and expanded at Cambridge, his character deepening and widening as thought elevated him and suffering became his lot.

Yet, all this time, George Herbert's heart was not wholly in his reading; he hungered for the town, for courtly talk and compliment, and all the arts of graceful living. He writes—

> " Whereas my birth and spirit rather took
>   The way that takes the town,
>   Thou didst betray me to a lingering book,
>   And wrap me in a gown."

At Wilton House Laud met him as he was thus

doubting, and they had a secret conversation, the
upshot of which was, that Herbert sent to Salisbury
at once for a tailor to cut out his canonical clothes,
and was privately ordained by the Archbishop.

We do not know exactly what passed : it may
have been nothing more than the magic influence
of a brisk decided mind upon a more wavering
one, crystallizing the thoughts still in solution into
sudden firmness ; but I cannot believe that this
was all.

If we consider in which direction Herbert's
temptations lay — to splendour and grace and
worldly magnificence,—knowing, as we do, that he
was withheld to a great degree by a certain dread
of degradation from adopting the profession of
the country parson, we cannot doubt what occurred.
Laud, no doubt, sketched out his great design so
as to dazzle the eyes of his hearer. He drew the
majestic Church in her royal state, moving on
through the ages. He spoke of her pomp, her
ceremonial, her princely claims,—not, I think, in an
unworthy way ; not as a bait to land a tempting
prey—for there is no doubt that George Herbert
was, from a worldly point of view, a convert well
worth securing—but as giving to this receptive
mind a true picture of the ancient splendours, of
the huge possibilities of the Church.

It was enough to turn the wavering scale. George Herbert, attracted perhaps by the " Beautiful Gate of the Temple," passed in, and became a true and devoted poor servant of Christ.

Laud little knew what he was doing when he drew aside the slender graceful young courtier, with his dreamy eyes and silky hair, into the gallery at Wilton, and paced to and fro with him, speaking in his sharp eager tones, with quick active gestures as his manner was, of all the glorious inheritance of the Church of Christ. He little knew that that gentle student was to glorify his dearly loved mistress far more effectually than he ever did himself, and by a far more delicate weapon : he little knew that George Herbert was to set on the Church that mark of singular and solemn refinement that has won to her so many high natures and sensitive souls,—that refinement " so perfect," as has been beautifully said, "that it requires an initiation to comprehend it."

Laud was to come into spiritual contact with another strange and characteristic figure, too. Nicholas Ferrar, like George Herbert, was to be his spiritual son.

A few miles from Huntingdon, passing out of that comfortable little town, of which Laud himself had been Archdeacon, by the Northern Road, leaving

Hinchinbrook, the seat of the Cromwells, now Lord Sandwich's, on the right, the road, after winding among broad flat water-meadows, at last runs up into low hills, into country quiet from horizon to horizon. After some little belts of woodland and isolated spinneys, a farm-road dips down to the left ; at the end of this stands a large, prosperous-looking farmhouse, and to the left, below a space of tumbled pasture-ground, on the skirts of and backed by a little overgrown wood, a lonely chapel, with a quaint Renaissance front of gray stone. The whole place has an unutterable air of retirement and quiet about it : the birds in the woods, the cries of children, the tinkle of sheep-bells in the pastures on the opposite slope, the sound of waggons grumbling along the rough farm-roads— these are the only sounds audible.

This is the chapel of Little Gidding—this, and the gray gravestones of Collets and Ferrars, are the only relics of that community whose pure precise life has been lately depicted with such sympathetic accuracy in the pages of " John Inglesant." Manor and groves and latticed walks are gone ; but standing in the obscure light of the sanctuary, so seemly and lovingly restored, or outside by the stream, with the shadow of the chapel on the grass, it is possible for us to pass in fancy back for a moment

or two to the ideal life that held rule there two
centuries ago. Ay, and it is good too! though the
tendency of the age—and who will blame it?—is
to say sadly that it was nothing more than a holy
error, a beautiful mistake.

The community was founded by Nicholas Ferrar,
a young man of burgher origin, trained to be a
physician, but of a retired devotional soul. After
some wanderings and much inclination towards the
Church of Rome, he came to the conclusion that
he need not step outside the English Church to
find the mystical sentiment for which he thirsted.

A character with a single-minded enthusiasm,
the offspring of his age, is sure to find a few devoted
followers. As could have been expected, his disciples were for the most part women; but the fame
and sweetness of the little world attracted many
to visit it—among others Crashaw, the religious
poet, afterwards a Roman Catholic and Canon of
Loretto, and George Herbert.

The object of the life was devotion. There was
to be a perpetual sacrifice of intercession : day and
night were divided into watches, and prayer went
up continually. There were offices at each of the
canonical hours, and full daily services. Besides
this, the children of the neighbourhood were schooled,
the sick visited, and the distressed comforted. The

simple rustics were encouraged to come and tell
their tale of sorrow : food and clothing were distributed.

The tendency of the house was ascetic. Nicholas
Ferrar stinted himself in food and sleep ; he slept
in a frieze gown, on the boards, and at midnight
arose to give thanks. The Collet and Ferrar
maidens—his cousins and friends whom he had
attracted to him, and who went by quaint titles,
emblematical of Christian virtues, such as the
Patient, the Submiss—watched likewise. The
pleasure, even rapture, they found in this utter
self-abnegation is unmistakable.

Mr. Shorthouse makes the recluses of Gidding,
with innocent curiosity, in their recreation hour,
ask John Inglesant all kinds of questions about the
Court, and especially about the king. It is a most
dramatic touch ; they slip off so naturally the
devotional cilice, and appear in their true characters
as little pitchers. They were soon to see him. On a
royal progress to Newmarket, the king and Court
turned aside to visit the place. " The King and
the Prince, the Palsgrave of Bohemia, the Duke of
Lennox, and divers other nobles staying a morning
there." There was an inspection of the whole place.
The young lords went into the buttery and there
found apple-pies and cheese-cakes, and came out

with pieces in their hands, laughing, to the prince :
" Sir, will your Highness taste?" Charles expressed
especial admiration at the neatness of the alms-
houses : " God's blessing upon the founder of it.
Time was,"—to the poor roving Palsgrave,—" you
would have thought such a lodging not amiss."
The Palsgrave thought so too, and said as much.
The king took out five pieces of gold and gave
them for the poor widows' benefit : he had won
them, the night before, at cards. " It is all I have,
else they should have more ; tell them to pray for
me." At last they left reluctantly. " It is late ;
the sun is going down ; we must away." So their
horses were brought to the door. The king mount-
ing, those of the family, men and women, all kneeled
down and heartily prayed God to bless and defend
him from all his enemies. " Pray—pray for my
speedy return," said his Majesty, taking off his hat.
The thought of those simple holy souls praying for
him affected him ; he was grave as he rode away.

Young Nicholas Ferrar, nephew of the elder
Nicholas, came up to Court after this with presents
for the king. Part of the industry at Gidding was
the making of diatessarons, or continuous gospel
narratives, selected from the four Evangelists, out
of two Testaments cut into pieces and pasted on
books, and afterwards deftly adorned with pictures

and bound, by the same skilful hands, in green or
purple velvet, with broad strings edged with gold
lace. " Glorious ! " "jewels ! " " precious stones ! "
"crystals!" said the king, and paid many other
strange compliments. He even read and annotated them in his own hand, as his custom was.

On this occasion the young Nicholas came up to
London, and went to Lambeth as directed. When
he was taken to the Archbishop he knelt down,
craved his blessing, and kissed his hand. " My
Lord embraced him very lovingly, took him up,
and after some salutes " proceeded to business : he
examined the books, now become an annual institution, and expressed himself well pleased with
them. This was the Wednesday before Easter.
The next day, being Maundy Thursday, the Archbishop took him to Whitehall. The king was in a
presence chamber, standing by a fire, chatting to
some nobles. " What," he said to the Archbishop,
" have you brought with you those rarities and
jewels you told me of?" " Yes, here is the young
gentleman and his works." He led him by the hand
to the king. The case was opened and the volumes
displayed ; the chief was the Gospel in eight.
languages, all young Nicholas's work. There were
courtly exclamations of astonishment and interest
on all sides. Charles kindly promised to send the

lad to Oxford at his own expense, and the audience was presently at an end ; Nicholas was taken away to dine with the younger lords.

When young Nicholas had been ushered out, "What a pity," said the king, "is that impediment in his tongue!" Laud characteristically said that he could not agree ; had he had the full use of his natural tongue, he would not have gained so many written ones. The Earl of Holland recommended the use of pebbles in the mouth. But the king had tried that, and had found it no good ; singing was the only cure—he must learn singing.

He had brought a book for the little Prince Charles as well ; this was illustrated with painted pictures which pleased the children. "Will you not make me such another fine book?" said the little Duke of York ; "do." Most certainly, his Grace "should have one without fail." "But how long will it be before I have it?" "Very soon." "Yes, but how long will that be? Tell the ladies at Gidding to be quick." Pretty childish gossip this. One cannot help wondering what place in the childish memories this scene took for the two future kings.

When Nicholas set off next day from Lambeth, the Archbishop had a touching interview with him. He reminded him of the king's promise ; he told

him that his Majesty wished to have a polyglot
of the New Testament in twenty-four languages.
This was to be the lad's work; he should have the
help of all the learning of the nation at his command. " The youth, kneeling down, took the Archbishop by the hand, and kissed it. The Archbishop
took him up in his arms, and laid his hand upon
his cheek, and earnestly besought God Almighty
to bless him, and increase all graces in him, and fit
him every day more and more for an instrument of
His glory here upon earth, and a saint in heaven.
'God bless you! God bless you! I have told your
father what is to be done for you after the holidays.
God will provide for you better than your father
can. God bless you and help you!'"

And God did provide. Poor boy, he died in a
few months, called to some more unseen work,
more high than polyglots, though sanctioned by
the king's command. A more pathetic scene has
seldom so truly been told. Would we had more
of that human Laud, breaking through the dry
official crust! If only he had shown this tenderness
oftener, how far more we should have loved him!

But it was not only to the votaries of the Church
on her æsthetic side that the sympathies of the
Primate were given: we must not forget that he
was brought into very close and intimate contact

with that school of English Rationalists that sprang
to life so vigorously in his day.

Lucius Cary, Viscount Falkland, has been made
too famous and familiar by Mr. Matthew Arnold's
well-known essay, a model of biographical study-
writing, for me to enter into his life here.

It will be enough to say that he was one of the
most sympathetic thinkers of the age, the chosen
friend of all the more enlightened spirits whom he
grouped round him, not so much from his wit or
his grasp of thought, though his mind was quick
and subtle, as from his unique power, and still
more unique desire of entering, or trying to enter,
into what a man had to say.

At Great Tew, a manorhouse not far from
Oxford, he held his delightful sessions, Oxford
scholars coming and going as they would, unknown
to their host, who used his wealth, as it is so rarely
used, to secure hospitality at any moment and for
any number of unexpected comers, without the
usual accompaniment of any domestic confusion.

Here Chillingworth and the " Ever-memorable "
Hales were wont to come ; and it is the former
of these whose intimacy with Laud must be held
to be, considering their respective opinions and the
warmth with which they advanced them, a strong
testimony to large-mindedness on both sides.

Chillingworth, son of a mayor of Oxford, was Laud's own godson. He was elected Fellow of Trinity at the age of twenty-six. " No drudge at his books," says Aubrey, " but a keen argumentative scholar, fond of sharpening his wits at the expense of any 'cod's head' he could get to enter into discussion with him."

At first he fell under the suspicion of having acted as Laud's *delator* or informer at Oxford. It is known that he sent him a weekly budget of intelligence, reporting conversations, notable sayings, anything in fact that indicated in which way opinion moved. In one of these letters he probably told him (though, as the document does not exist, it is only conjecture) of some extravagant expression about the Duke of Buckingham's murder, in praise of Felton, that had fallen from the lips of Alexander Gill, who was usher of St. Paul's School, and had had the teaching of Milton. These opinions had been stated in the course of a confidential conversation, of rather a roystering kind, with a few intimate friends in the cellar of Trinity College. " He was sorry," he had said, " that Felton had deprived him of the honour of doing that brave act."

For this, Gill was condemned to be branded, lose his place and his ears, and pay a heavy fine ; and though fine and corporal punishment were remitted by the king, it is rather a revolting story : it argues that if Chillingworth was nothing more than indiscreet in writing it, Laud was nothing less than unscrupulous in using it.

The next act in Chillingworth's life was a stirring one; he became convinced by the arguments of the Jesuit Fisher, whom Laud afterwards condescended to refute in a lengthy and nearly unreadable folio, that there was a want of continuity about the Protestant Church.* Chillingworth's was a mere logical conversion. In 1630 he went to the Jesuit College at Douay, where he was urged to put in writing a kind of Apologia, to indicate the line along which he had moved. This was a singularly indiscreet attempt. They did not foresee the result. In the course of the investigations which it necessitated, Chillingworth was led to the conclusion that it had been a hasty step ; and a series of kindly letters from Laud led to his quitting Douay for Oxford, where, in 1634, he published a book containing his reasons for becoming a Romanist, accompanied by an elaborate refutation ; and at last, in 1637, appeared, with the

* Fisher, alias Percy, was a dangerous man ; he converted the Countess of Buckingham, the duke's mother, to Rome, and very nearly the duke himself.

sanction of the University Press, his most important work, "The Religion of Protestants a Safe
Way to Salvation." It was originally an answer
to a Jesuit pamphlet, and suffers much from its
extraneous form. A second edition was called for
within five months ; and it was generally regarded
as a book of consummate ability.

He had scruples about subscription ; but Laud
overcame them, and made him Canon of Salisbury
and master of a hospital at Leicester. We hear
little more of him, except that, having accompanied
the king's forces as chaplain, he devised a siege-
engine, in the form of a *testudo*, before Gloucester ;
but before it was successfully tried the siege was
raised. Being left ill at Arundel, he fell into
the hands of the Roundheads on the fall of the
Castle, and died at Chichester, pestered to death,
it was said, by the Puritan officers, who insisted on
disputing with and exhorting him, when he was
far too ill for such treatment. At his funeral
a Puritan divine, named Cheynell, had the ex-
quisitely bad taste to fling a copy of his great
book on to his coffin as the earth was thrown in,
expressing a fervent wish that "it might rot
with its author and see corruption."

With the "Ever-memorable" Hales, too, Fellow
of Eton, Laud came in contact. He was another of

the same school, and owed his title to his extreme brilliancy as a conversationalist, and his sympathetic listening powers.

His interview with the Archbishop is dramatic and entertaining to the highest degree. Hales, for the satisfaction of some weak-minded friend, wrote out his views on schism, treating the whole subject with a humorous contempt for Church authority. This little tract got privately printed, and a copy fell into Laud's hands (as, indeed, what dangerous matter did not ?), which having read and marked, he instantly sent for his recalcitrant subaltern, to be rated and confuted and silenced. It is wonderfully characteristic of Laud, both in the idea and in the method of carrying it out. Mr. Hales came, says Heylyn, about nine o'clock on a summer morning to Lambeth, with considerable heart-sinking, no doubt. The Archbishop had him out into the garden, giving orders that they were on no account to be disturbed. The bell rang for prayers, to which they went by the garden door into the chapel, and out again till dinner was ready, hammer and tongs all the time ; then they fell to again : but Lord Conway and several other persons of distinction having meantime arrived, the servants were obliged to go and warn the disputants how the time was going. It was now about four in the afternoon.

" So in they came," says Heylyn, " highly coloured
and almost panting for want of breath ; enough to
shew that there had been some heats between them
not then fully cooled." The two little cassocked
figures (both were very small men), with their fresh
complexions, set off by tiny mustachios and im-
perials, such as Churchmen wore, pacing up and
down under the high elms of the garden, and
arguing to the verge of exhaustion, is a wonderful
little picture.

Hales afterwards confessed to Heylyn that it had
been dreadful. " He had been ferreted," he said,
" from one hole to another, till he was resolved to
be orthodox and declare himself a true son of the
Church of England, both for doctrine and discipline."

Laud evidently saw the mettle of the man with
whom he had to deal, and what a very dangerous
rational opponent he was ; so he made him his own
chaplain, and got the king to offer him a canonry
at Windsor, in such a way that refusal, much to
Hales' distaste, was out of the question, thus binding him to silence in a manner that would make
further speech ungracious. " And so," said Hales,
quietly grumbling at his wealthy loss of independence, " I had a hundred and fifty more pounds
a year than I cared to spend."

It has been the fashion lately to speak of this interview as if Hales had been merely fooling the pompous chaplain. But though, of course, we must not take the words too literally, especially from such ironical lips, yet I have no doubt that, from a logical point of view, Laud had the best of the argument. Hales was certainly silenced ; Principal Tulloch believes he was not convinced.

The real truth is, that he probably did not dare to reveal how dissident his own position was from Laud's. Hales had advanced further towards scepticism than Chillingworth, and it is hardly possible to conceive that a man who was a Rationalist by thirty had gone no further by the time he was fifty ; but I can well imagine him shrinking from laying bare his wanderings before the keen ear and the piercing tongue of his sturdy and argumentative Metropolitan.

It is impossible to believe that, had Hales and Chillingworth been born in these later days, they would have ever taken upon themselves the ministry of the Church ; it is hardly conceivable, indeed, that they would have remained within her communion. They were the predecessors of the Agnostic movement of the present time. When Revelation was taken for granted as much as geology is now, it was impossible to stray very far from the fold; even Lord Herbert of Cherbury, and the Deists assailed Inspiration with no certain hand. Hales and Chillingworth were really the first who nibbled at the question of the limits of the credible. Unfortunately, Science has thrown such a sudden glare upon the question of Revelation and its limitations, that the true vision has for a time been drowned in excess of light. Hales and Chillingworth had no external illumination, but they were far too clear-sighted not to discern directly the fact, that perfect truth is probably not the exact property of any school or any age.

If there were reason to think that Laud saw the direction in which their doubts tended, or the ultimate end of their reasonings, his position towards them would do the greatest credit both to his clearness of vision and to his tolerance. But it is far more probable that he considered them to be little more than a pronounced variation from the true line, and much more capable of being ruled straight again than the cross-grained headstrong Puritan.

Thus, here as elsewhere, we are forced to the conclusion that he feared and hated an unruly and coarse earnestness far more genuinely than a silent, subtle, but infinitely more deadly perversion.

The great instrument by which Laud made himself felt was the Court of High Commission for ecclesiastical causes, and the Star Chamber, so called from the ornamented ceiling of the room in which it met. This latter was a court of summary jurisdiction, dealing with all offences against public order, from libels down to Sunday pastimes. By the former court, the preaching of all debated doctrinal questions was limited to high dignitaries of the Church. Clergymen were deprived for gospel preaching; surplices, "whites" so-called, and all ceremonies offensive to Puritan taste were rigorously enforced. Among other systems, the elaborate system of lecturers, devised to serve Puritan ends, was crushed. Lecturers were a sort of unattached clergy, with no cure of souls, who preached, mostly in town parishes, the subjects so dear to the hard-headed farmers and traders of the day—so hateful to Laud. These were suppressed by the High Commission under Laud's presidency; or rather their subjects were taken away, and they were forbidden to preach till they had read the Service of the Church. The country gentlemen came to the rescue, and took them in as chaplains: Laud stepped forward and forbade chaplains to all but noblemen. Then the Puritans tried to buy livings for their favourites: Laud forbade the combined purchase of patronage. It is curious that,

with all this zeal for reform, it never occurred to
him to consider pluralities unsatisfactory. Bowing
to the altar on entering a church was recommended.
Kneeling was enforced at the Communion. Again,
the feeling of the country was setting in the direction of a stricter observance of Sunday. The
Court was in favour of games and amusements.
Parliament, on the other hand, promulgated an
order against the profanation of the Sabbath.
The Chief Justice, Richardson, directed that this
should be read from the pulpit on a certain Sunday,
by every clergyman in England. Laud was furious
at this, and complained to the king, who sent a
message to Richardson requiring him to revoke the
order at the next assizes. This Richardson
merely disregarded. At the summer assizes he
received another requisition. He then revoked the
order, in a disrespectful speech, indicating that he
was acting under compulsion. He was immediately
summoned before a Committee of the Council,
where Laud rated him soundly for disobedience,
and forbade him ever to ride the western circuit
again. He left the room with tears in his eyes.
"I have been almost choked," he said, "by a pair
of lawn sleeves." Such scenes were not of uncommon occurrence. Laud then issued a counter-
order that the decree in favour of Sunday pastimes

should be read, and deprived four hundred and twenty clergy for disobeying this.

These dreary scenes of sifting unsatisfactory evidence, censuring, and sentencing were occasionally relieved. A poor schoolmaster from Norfolk, Brabourne by name, accused of Socinian opinions, was so paternally exhorted by Laud, that he professed himself converted. Dame Eleanor Davies, a religious maniac, furnished, perhaps, the most amusing incident of all. This lady, who has been already alluded to in the Strafford correspondence, uttered a prophecy that the Archbishop would not outlive the 5th of November, 1633 ; for which, and other wild statements, she was had before the Commission.

The poor creature based her power of prophecy upon the fact that the letters of her name made, in an anagram, the words " REVEAL, O DANIEL." The Bishops and divines present gravely began to argue with her, and quote Scripture, and express themselves shocked. All this time, Lamb, Dean of Arches, was seen to be busy with his pen ; after a few minutes he looked up. " Madam," he said, " I see you build much on anagrams, and I have found one which I think will fit you," and he read out the words, " NEVER SO MAD A LADIE," and passed her the paper. There was an outburst of laughter from the whole court, and the poor lady retired in such confusion that, as Heylyn says, she afterwards "grew wiser, or was less regarded."

I will mention here, as an instance of the proceedings of the Star Chamber, an incident which really belongs to a later date. Prynne, a Puritan lawyer of good position, published a book called "Histriomastix," a general attack on the stage and its demoralizing effects on the nation. The book to us is incredibly ludicrous and disproportionate. Like Draco's Code, it uses up so distilled an essence of invective on such practices as decking houses at Christmas with evergreens, on hunting, music, and false hair, that it can find nothing worse to say about graver lapses. The mere extent and detailedness of the criticism destroys the value of the whole. But the queen was, if not mentioned by name, at all events unmistakably included in the condemnation. Charles sent the book to the Star Chamber, who thought fit to inflict on Prynne a hopelessly large fine, to pillory him, cut off both his ears, burn his books, strike off his name from the Inns of Court and the register of Oxford. This was tyranny ; the book was far too absurd to be taken so seriously. No rational man could have approved of it. The effect of the punishment was, that a great many rational men looked grave over the acts of the counsellors of the king.

In the following June Prynne seized the first opportunity that presented itself, to write a libellous letter to Laud, which Laud sent to the Attorney-General, Noy.

Noy thereupon sent for Prynne, and asked him whether the letter was in his handwriting or not. Prynne answered that he could not tell unless he could see the letter. As soon as it was put into his hands, Noy happening to turn his back, he tore it up, and threw it out of the window, saying that it, at least, should never rise in judgment against him.

Thus, the only proof of the misdemeanour being destroyed, there was no remedy; and Laud stepped forward, and said that he did not wish to press the matter. It apparently caused him genuine surprise to find that Prynne felt no remorse for his previous course of action, and that the punishment, instead of producing a salutary effect, had hardened him. So little did he know of men.

In the midst of this perpetual and absorbing work Abbot had died, at Ford, in retirement. Whereupon Laud merely moved his books to Lambeth. He had been too long the virtual Archbishop to feel the change.

For a superstitious mind, his tenure did not begin
well; his coach and horses were overturned in the
Lambeth ferry-boat, the coach remaining at the
bottom. He himself writes of a heaviness over-
hanging him ever since his nomination to the place.
But there was no outward sign of dismay. The
last section described his negative policy with
respect to religion—the system that he strove to
eradicate. His action at Lambeth will give some
idea of the positive doctrine that he laboured to
introduce. The chapel, as he found it, was typical
of the state to which the science of worship had
been reduced by a gradual process since the
Reformation. It was a whitewashed room with
plain glazed windows. Abbot, by breaking down
the organ, had put the seal of Calvinism upon it.
" It did lie so nastily," said the new Archbishop,
" that I was much ashamed to see it, and could not
resort unto it without disdain." Under Laud's
hands the place blossomed afresh; with his own
hands he pieced out the fragments of broken glass
that remained, and restored the rest. The stately
screen he erected is still in its place; the very
altar rails are preserved in the chapel-screen at
Addington. Of course Laud's windows were broken
by the soldiers of the Commonwealth. But by a
furious freak of fate the present chapel windows,

with their mottoes from the Vulgate, are the precise
reproduction of Laud's. When the chapel was
restored ten years ago, it was remembered that
an exact description of the windows with their
legends was one of the articles of Laud's indict-
ment that was still preserved ; and by this Hard-
man worked. Under Laud's reforming hand, the
organ and the choir came back ; the copes of the
chaplains, the arras worked with sacred scenes, the
credence, the consecrated vessels, the silver candle-
sticks, the bowing at the name of Jesus, the stately
ritual,—all these were there.

In Prynne's so-called "Life of Laud" there is a
little plan of a chapel, purporting to be the chapel
at Abergwili.

It will be remembered that Laud's first act on
coming there was to build and consecrate a chapel.
That he dedicated it to St. John and consecrated
it on the day of the Decollation was detestable to
Prynne.

But the unprejudiced reader would, I think, be
surprised, on looking at the plan, to see two small
round vessels indicated as standing on a platform
or footpace, with a "musique table," in the centre
of the chapel, between the litany desk and the
lectern, and to see, on referring to the plan, that
these are respectively marked the censer, and

the *navicula*, or vessel for holding the frankincense.

Otherwise, the chapel is very ordinary: there is the altar railed off, a credence, lectern, litany desk, as I have said, and return stalls for the clergy. There is ˙subjoined a long list of copes and veils, and very elaborate altar furniture of flagons, basons, chalices, etc.

Laud's allusion to this, in his defence, is a very curious one. He becomes ironical. He is glad to learn, he says, that his estate was so plentiful at that time, that he could have afforded such sumptuous surroundings.

The truth is, that it is an excellent instance of Prynne's shameless malevolence; if it is mere carelessness, it is carelessness so culpable in such a matter as the trial of a public man as to be very nearly as criminal as deliberate perjury. The fact in reality being that Laud, when building his chapel, wrote to Bishop Lancelot Andrews for a description of the chapel at Farnham. One of the chaplains drew out a rough plan, which was enclosed. Thus the plan was the plan of the chapel at Farnham, which, for nearly twenty years, had been in different hands, and under a totally different *régime.*

I confess that it is still surprising to hear that

incense was in common use in Bishop Andrews's
chapel; and it appears from the evidence that
wafers were used there instead of bread, which
will be to many an unfamiliar fact.

With these proclivities, however, it was no
wonder, in a land dry with Calvinism, that, as
Laud notes in his Diary immediately after his
nomination to Canterbury, "there came one
secretly to me by night, and proffered me, as with
authority, a Cardinal's hat, and the same offer was
shortly after repeated. To whom I made answer,
that I must first see Rome other than it was." And
the answer was a very genuine one. Laud was
hardly nearer Rome than he was to Calvinism.
He was far too real an Erastian at heart, far too
earnest a believer in the interdependence of Church
and State to lie down either with the Pope or
Luther. Nothing can be a greater mistake than
to believe Laud to have been a Romanist at heart,
restrained, by motives of timidity or prudence,
from declaring himself. Montague and Gardiner
were instances of that. Whatever his faults were,
Laud was no hypocrite. If he had believed the
Pope right, to the Pope he would have gone.
Perhaps he hated Protestantism the worse of the
two, for he loved neither the soul of it nor the
clothes it wore; whereas, he was well satisfied with

the trappings of Romanism : but its arrogance of spirituality was quite outside his field of view. Compare the feeling at Rome with which the news of his death was received. They evidently did not regard him as their friend.

John Evelyn was at Rome at the time, and in the company of several of the English Romanists and Jesuit fathers. The news arrived, and copies of Laud's speech on the scaffold were circulated. They received the news with satisfaction ; they commented on the speech with contempt, and evidently regarded his death as the removal of a great obstacle out of their path, the suppression of a dangerous rival. And yet his popish tendencies were the only serious charges brought against him. His definition of the Church of England would doubtless have been very much what a High Anglican of the present century would give—an uncorrupt Apostolic section ; but he lacked the sympathy and toleration for the profession of which the better Anglicans are now so conspicuous.

CHAPTER IX.

ONE of the achievements of which Laud speaks
with the most profound satisfaction was the fact
that he induced Charles to make Juxon, Bishop of
London, Lord High Treasurer. If Laud had been
a little more clear-sighted he would have felt that
the little increase of secular dignity it gave to the
Church was much more than counterbalanced by
the natural jealousy of ecclesiastical interference
that it suggested, and the uneasy suspicion that
the Church was aiming at a civil tyranny. It only
gave additional fuel to the flames.

Charles sent suddenly for the white staff, in the
middle of a council, and delivered it to Juxon. It
evidently took the councillors by surprise, though
there had been a rumour to that effect circulating
a few days before. Charles made a short speech,
in which he explained his reasons: discretion
and foresight were the qualities he wanted, if
they could be found in a conscientious man. This

combination he looked for among the clergy ; and Juxon, as having no children, and thus with no private motive to self-enrichment, was the best.

"No churchman," notes Laud, "has had it since Henry the Seventh's time. I pray God to bless him in it. Now if the Church will not hold themselves up under God, I can do no more."

The elation to which Laud owns was general. Mr. Garrard, Master of the Charterhouse, writes to Strafford, " The Clergy are so high since the joining of the white sleeves with the white staff, that there is much talk of having a Secretary a Bishop, and a Chancellor of the Exchequer a Bishop, Dr. Bancroft. But this comes only from the Small Fry of the Clergy : little credit is given to it ; but it is observed that they swarm mightily at Court."

Laud had discovered, by inquiry, that a Treasurer could honestly make £7000 a year without degrading the Treasury or abusing his privileges ; that lately Treasurers, from mean private fortunes, had risen to the titles and estates of earls. If this was the case, a man with absolutely no personal motive would be a very useful servant for the king in his very impoverished condition.

Juxon's was an admirable appointment. He did his work quietly ; unlike Laud, was gentle and courteous with all, and never became a party man.

When he resigned it a few years later, he left it with universal respect. Even Prynne allowed that he had done fairly well.

Juxon was a *protégé* of Laud's, one of the St. John's men whom he had drawn up with him. We know he had an enthusiastic admiration for Laud. He succeeded him at Lambeth, and in the guard-room their portraits hang side by side,—Juxon's evidently painted so as to be the precise counterpart of Laud's, the dress and pose precisely similar, so that they might hang somewhere side by side, or flank some central portrait—the fact is unmistakable.

Laud's work was now prodigious; he ruled the Church with a rod of iron. No recalcitrant was unknown to him; no schismatic writings made their appearance but he read and marked them. He was President of the Court of High Commission, First Minister of the Crown, a member of the Treasury Commission and the Foreign Council. Such was his amazing energy, that the very merchants who memorialized him owned him their master in his grasp of Economic problems. He was Chancellor of Oxford and Dublin Universities. His correspondence with the Vice-Chancellor and Senate of the former fills a large folio volume. Of the detailedness of his scrutiny we have some

I

idea when we remember that in one letter he pre-
scribes the dress of the undergraduates of noble
birth, and in another desires the abolition of the
Westminster dinner. He administered his own
diocese without a suffragan ; he corresponded with
Strafford in Ireland ; he entertained largely ; he
was much at Court ; he preached frequently. And
all this work is both comprehensive and detailed :
he did not sketch bold lines of organization and
leave the filling-in to others ; he devised, organized,
and executed, single-handed and indomitable.

The Pope, it used to be said, had longer arms
than any prince in Christendom. The fingers of
the Archbishop, which had long been groping un-
comfortably from Land's End to John o' Groat's,
at last crept into Scotland. On the whole the
Scots had taken Episcopacy with a good grace.
But there arose a sinister murmuring when vacancy
after vacancy on the Scottish Bench began to be
filled with English Laudian prelates; and it became
still louder when Charles began to emphasize their
political importance by calling them to the Council
Board of Scotland, and appointing them to high
offices of State. Spottiswoode, of St. Andrew's,
was made Lord Chancellor. Perhaps if he had
stopped there all might have been well. But he
went farther : instigated by Laud, whose disgust

had been stirred on his two Scottish visits, with James and Charles respectively, by the repulsive aspect of the Churches, the king turned his thoughts to the restitution of a decent worship in Scotland. James had told Laud roughly that he did not know the temper of the people. Charles did not care about that. Laud had already informed the Scotch that the Reformation in Scotland had been little better than a deformation. Charles resolved to give them a good Prayer Book. It was drawn up by Laud; printed and reprinted till it reached typographical excellence. The last copy, still in the Lambeth library, received the final annotations of Laud. His additions are even more pronounced than those of the English ritual : e.g. he reinstated the eastward position. A decree was despatched ordering two copies to be purchased for every parish.

On the 24th of July, 1638, the book was to come into use. The attempt was not successful. At Edinburgh not only were the windows broken and the entire service made inaudible by groans and cries, but the Dean had a three-legged stool thrown at his head by one Jenny Geddes, and the Bishop had to be guarded home by the military. Then Charles's true nature came out. No attempt was made to discover why the book was so obnoxious.

It did not occur to Charles that the advantages of a seemly ritual were more than counterbalanced by the opposition and hatred which the innovation produced. To make concessions to a popular outcry, especially when it had expressed itself by brutal and rebellious acts, was alien to his nature. Edinburgh must be punished, and a peremptory order was despatched removing the Council and Courts of Session to Glasgow.

The effect was prodigious : it meant the entire collapse of the place. Edinburgh was not a trading town ; its industries depended on its position as capital. That a nation should be outraged by the capricious whim of a distant sovereign and a Pope of Canterbury, was too great a blow. A remonstrance was forwarded to Charles, but without effect. Into the progress of the dispute we cannot enter in detail. It is enough to say that the immediate result was the signing of the Scottish Covenant ; the signing of the Scottish Covenant was the spark that kindled the rebellion. The action of the king, the action of Laud are unpardonable. The fact was, that they did not realize that they had anything to do but to govern ; they did not understand that the democracy had but just become conscious, blindly but surely, of its thews and sinews. This was their fundamental mistake ; on this rock they made shipwreck.

The candid historian is compelled to interpret this as an instance of the strange want of political sagacity and sympathetic foresight in Laud. Not so his Catholic supporters. " Happy is the servant," they say, "who is interrupted at such a task, going so intently about the Father's business."

One of the most piteous and humiliating spectacles of Charles's reign is the perpetual and unavailing cry for money that characterized it all along. Pledging the crown jewels, the sale of royal plate—these had been the first expedients, soon exhausted ; enforced knighthood, meaning fees to the exchequer and fines for defaulters, heavy taxation of Roman Catholic residents in Great Britain, ship-money, are the later stages of the disorder. Into this political turmoil it is impossible to enter ; we have to confine ourselves to the ecclesiastical aspect of affairs. With the Scottish Rebellion, Church politics, Church bickerings are drowned in the growing rumour of civil war. Under all this Laud worked quietly, blindly, ejecting recalcitrant curates, enjoining altar rails, silencing lecturers. It is a strange thing to find Laud thus busily at work, never dreaming of what was over him, with rebellion knocking at the doors. He had one or two warnings. A mob of five hundred besieged Lambeth for two hours at midnight. He had been informed of it, and had fortified the

house so that no harm was done; and one of the
ringleaders was hung, drawn, and quartered, a few
days after, at Southwark. A flood of libels poured
in upon him; they were even placed in his book
at chapel, and pinned on to his clothes at night.
The titles of these would be ridiculous, did they
not stand for so much real obloquy and hatred.
" Beelzebub's triumphant Arch to adorn his vic-
tories," and so forth. Laud's comments on these
papers is pathetic : he notes many of them in his
Diary; they are to be found among the Lambeth
papers, annotated in his own hand. He is genuinely
unable to understand the cause or the extent of
his extreme unpopularity. The thought that he
has been oppressive, tyrannical, or even unsympathetic never crosses his mind ; he speaks like a man
convinced of rectitude, sincerely troubled at being
misunderstood, bearing his reproach quietly because
he feels it to be the human reward for duty done.
Hard and dull he may be thought ; but it is impossible not to feel, in the later pages of his Diary,
that he was good.

In November, 1640, the Long Parliament gathered
at Westminster. One by one the illegal acts of the
tyranny were cancelled. Prynne and his fellow
martyrs were released in triumph : the storm had
broken at last.

Then Strafford fell. His fall emboldened all the rising party. The king delayed all day, asked many an opinion, and finally signed the warrant with tears of rage and despair. Laud, asking for a short recess, apparently invariably granted to the two Houses during the meeting of Convocation, was told in the House of Lords that the presence of the Bishops was not necessary to their deliberations ; whereupon he rejoined that he had merely asked it of courtesy. It was grudgingly granted. But in the House of Commons there was more of a scene. Episcopacy was solemnly condemned. On the day on which Strafford's articles of impeachment were read, Charles sitting on the throne to hear them, Laud's impeachment was voted in the House of Commons. A week before he had found, on entering his study, as he records, quite unsuspicious of the danger, his own portrait—the portrait that I have already described—with the string broken, lying on its face on the ground. " I pray God it portend no evil." A month later, December 18th, he was impeached of high treason before the Upper House by the Scottish Commissioners, as an incendiary, under which general term were included all whose action was supposed in any way to have engendered revolution. "I was presently committed to the Gentleman Usher," he writes ; " but was permitted to go in his company to my house at Lambeth, for a book or two to read in, and such papers as pertained to my defence. I stayed at Lambeth till the evening, to avoid the gazing of the people. I went to evening prayer in my chapel. The Psalms of the day, xciii. and xciv., and chap. l. of Isaiah, gave me great comfort. God make me worthy of it and fit to receive it ! As I went to my barge hundreds of my poor neighbours stood there and prayed for my safety and return to my house. For which I bless God and them." I know of few authentic scenes which combine such tragic and pathetic elements—the long, restless day spent in the well-known house, musing over the sudden snapping off of all designs and treasured conceptions. It is not probable that he anticipated death, but it is certain that he expected to be sequestrated from his Arch-bishopric. We may stop to wonder a little over the thoughts of the busy self-willed man at such a crisis—so sure that he had been doing God's work, and yet so irresistibly arrested ; and then the fami-liar household routine not even interrupted ; the anxious wonderings and confabulations of chaplains, secretaries, and domestics ; the silence in the corridors, and evening chapel as the day closed in ; and the little active figure, the centre of so much life, moving to his place for the last time, almost broken down ; then the barge ordered as usual, and the crowd gathering at the gates—perhaps the only people in England who felt a spark of love for the hard lonely man.

Laud was sixty-seven when he was committed to prison—at first to a private house, but later to the Tower, for the severity of his gaolers increased. At the same time, he himself says that opportunities were constantly given him to make his escape ; and he hints that his escape, and his appearance in the character of a recreant, would have aided their cause. As it was, he was a troublesome prisoner ; they were nearly bound to put him to death, but they were aware that it could bear no construction except that of a political assassination. Charles's death might be excused on the ground of the bloodshed of which he was the direct cause ; but Laud was so very indirect a cause, and was, besides, a man of such blameless life, so devoted a son and Father of the Church, that the responsibility of ordering his execution was felt to be a serious one. His imprisonment made a great sensation on the Continent. He received a secret message from Grotius begging him to effect his escape ; to which he returned an affectionate but decided answer. Certainly he had not a touch of physical fear.

True souls do not seek martyrdom, but they do not decline it.   All this time there came to him news of the violence done to Lambeth—his house rifled, his chapel desecrated.   It was turned into a dining-room and a stable, its windows broken down.   All this time, though his powers were put in commission, the Parliament treated him as Archbishop, sending him peremptory orders to appoint such-and-such men to vacancies that occurred ; to which courteous refusals were returned.   He had free communication, too, with the king.

Then came the memorable scene when the day came for Strafford to suffer, and, desiring to have speech with Laud, was refused, but begged for his blessing as he went past to die.   Stern, unflinching friends they had been, these two, since they had first been drawn together in the councils of the king.   And a terrible interview it was.   Laud, through the barred window, gave his blessing as the procession moved on, and then fell to the ground *in animi deliquio*, as Heylyn says.   The only place where Laud becomes almost passionate in his denials is where he confutes the calumny that Strafford, on his last day, had cursed the Archbishop as the cause of all his troubles and ruin.

CHAPTER X.

BEFORE long it was determined to amass some testimony, if possible, against Laud ; it was thought that his papers would incriminate him in some treasonous correspondence—with the Church of Rome, it was hoped. The manner of the search was as brutal as it was unsuccessful. Prynne, as the accredited agent of the Parliament, came to the Tower at night with a file of musqueteers, entered Laud's room when he was in bed, and produced his warrant, wherein it was expressly said that his pockets should be searched, which was accordingly done. Prynne took away twenty-one bundles of letters prepared by Laud for his defence ; the Scottish Service-book, his Diary, and, last of all, his book of private devotions. "Nor could I get him," says Laud, "to leave the last, but he must needs see what passed between God and me : a thing, I think, scarce ever offered to any Christian. Among the papers," he continues, "he found a bundle of gloves. This bundle he was so careful to open as that he caused each glove to be looked into. Upon this I tendered him one pair of the gloves, which he refusing, I told him he might take them and fear no bribe, for he had already done me all the mischief he could, and I asked no favour of him. So he thanked me, took the gloves, bound up my papers, and went his way."

The sentence which Laud, as the representative of the Star Chamber, had pronounced, makes excusable a certain amount of energetic hatred on Prynne's part. But nothing can excuse or condone his subsequent proceedings. He sorted the letters, burning those that might be supposed to tell in Laud's favour. He cut with a knife and blotted out many entries of the same character in the Diary. In one place five pages are removed ; in another there is a great crescent-shaped burn, that extends over many pages, that looks as if it had been inflicted by a red-hot iron. This he called preparing the evidence. Finally, he published a selection, with notes, explaining, according to his own taste, the secret initials and ciphers in the book. It is needless to say that he understood these to mean gross immoralities in nearly every case. On the eighteenth, and last day of hearing, the Archbishop saw every Lord present with a new thin book in folio, in a blue coat. This was the published Diary.

The charges were frivolous. That of intended subversion of the laws of the kingdom, had a vague and ominous sound ; but it was merely supported by general assertions dealing with his method of administering justice, and his deliberate and evident purpose to support the king in whatever courses he adopted. The bringing in of popish superstition upon the Protestant religion was based upon the fact that he had been offered a Cardinal's hat, and upon a number of names of persons, supposed friends of Laud's, who had become Romanists, and upon whom he had either not used his influence so as to dissuade them, or used it in vain. This last charge he condescended to answer in detail.

The following may serve as specimens of the kind of facts, gravely alleged as criminal—nay, capital misdemeanours. Prynne first proceeds to describe what he gracefully calls his " kennel " at Lambeth. He stated that he had a Bible with a device of five wounds upon it, in his study, the gift of a devout lady ; that he had profane and popish pictures, such as the four doctrines of the Church, with a dove diffusing light—this picture is now the chief ornament of the great drawing-room at Lambeth; that he had a mass-book in his library, with popish pictures; that he had set a silver crucifix among the regalia at the Coronation; that he had repaired the stained glass at Lambeth.

The testimony was all incredibly loose. Richard Pember, a glazier, deposed that there was a picture of an old man, with a glory, in one window; he supposed it was meant for God the Father. Laud meekly shows that it was St. Matthias. Again, another witness stated that in one window there was represented an old man with a "budget" by his side, from which he was pulling Adam and Eve—a representation of the Creation, he supposed. The testimony is apparently genuinely given by a simple sort of person, and shows very curiously how people can persuade themselves of ocular facts by mere imagination.

Of course there was no such thing. And Laud almost laughingly shows the ludicrous impossibility of putting up such a conception of the scene.

Several of the charges relate to sharp offensive speech. A Mr. Vassal was called "Sirrah" by his Grace on one occasion. Laud cannot remember; he knows it is his custom to call gentlemen, such as Mr. Vassal, "Sir."

Again, they alleged that at the Coronation Laud,

acting as deputy for the Dean of Westminster, had
done his best to make the ceremony popish. He
had secretly introduced a silver crucifix upon the
altar, among the regalia. Laud himself could not
remember whether he had or not. He had caused
to be revived and used a prayer of Romish tendencies, which had been in disuse since the time
of Henry VI., and in which the following passage
occurred : " Let him obtain favour for his people,
like Aaron in the tabernacle, Elisha in the waters,
Zacharias in the temple ; give him Peter's key of
discipline, Paul's doctrine."

The following, a most curious and interesting
document for its insane malice and grotesque
exaggeration, is worthy of insertion here. It is
Prynne's account of the Consecration of St. Kathe-
rine Cree Church, in the city of London, on the
16th of January, 1630.

" The Bishop of London, Dr. Laud, came in the
morning about nine of the clock, in a pompous
manner, to Cree Church, accompanied by many
High Commissioners and Civilians : there being a
very great concourse of people to behold this
novelty. The Church doors were guarded with
many Halberdiers. At the Bishop's approaching
near the West Door of the Church, the Bishop's
hangbies [attendants] cried out in a loud voice,

'Open, open, ye everlasting doors, that the King of glory may come in;' and presently (as by miracle) the doors flew open, and the Bishop and three or four great Doctors entered in.

"As soon as they were in the Church, the Bishop fell down upon his knees with his eyes lifted up and his hands and armes spread abroad, uttering many words, and saying, 'The place is holy and this ground is holy. *In nomine, etc.*, I pronounce it holy:' and then he took up some of the earth or dust and threw it up into the aire (as the frantic persecuting Jews did, when they were raging mad against Paul). This was done several times. When they approached near to the Lord's table, the Bishop lowly ducked and bowed towards it some five or six times: and returning went about the Church in Procession on the inside thereof. . . . Then was read aloud 23 of Genesis . . . then another prayer, taken almost verbatim out of the Roman Pontifical. . . . After all this, the Bishop betook himself to sit under a Cloth of State in an aisle of the Chancel near the Communion table, and taking a written book in his hand (in imitation of the Roman Pontifical and the Council of Trent's decree) he pronounced ·many curses upon all that should prophane that holy place, . . . he then pronounced the like number of blessings to all those that had any hand in the culture, framing, or building of that holy and beautiful Church.

"After the Sermon, which was short, the Bishop and two fat Doctors consecrated and administered the Sacrament, with a number of bowings, duckings, and cringeings in manner following :—

"At first, when the Bishop approached neare the Communion Table he bowed with his nose very neare the ground some six or seven times ; then he came to one of the corners of the table, and there bowed himself three times ; then to the second, third, and fourth corners, bowing at each corner three times [which shows incidentally that the table must have been set out from the wall, as he evidently passed round, and so behind it]. But when he came to the side of the Table where the bread and wine was, he bowed himself seven times ; and then, after the reading of many prayers by himself and his two fat chaplains (which were with him, and all this while by him on their knees in Surplices, Hoods and Tippets), he himself came near the Bread which was cut and laid in a fine napkin, and peeped into it till he saw the bread (like a boy that peeped after a bird's nest in a bush) and presently clapped it down again and flew back a step or two, and then bowed very low three

K

times to it and the Table; then he came near and
opened the napkin again, and behaved as before:
then he laid his hand upon the Gilt cup which was
full of wine with a cover upon it. So soon as he
had pulled the Cup a little nearer to him, he let
the Cup go, flew back, and bowed again three
times towards it; then he came near again, and,
lifting up the cover of the Cup, peeped into it, and
seeing the wine, he let fall the cover on it again·
and flew nimbly back and bowed as before. After
these and many other Apish Antic gestures, he
himself received, and then gave the Sacrament to
some principal men only, they kneeling devoutly
near the table; after which, more prayers being
said, this scene and interlude ended."

Laud condescended to answer this tract in
detail, but no serious attention was paid to the
defence.

The whole conduct of the trial reflects the
greatest disgrace upon the Puritans. Each day
began by the charge being made; this lasted till
two o'clock. The Archbishop was then allowed
only two hours to prepare his defence—hardly time,
in some cases, to peruse the evidence; and no
counsel were admitted to him till after his answer.
His witnesses were not allowed to be sworn; and
one or more of the committee generally interrupted

him, or asked him fresh questions. At half-past
seven the proceedings of the day terminated. It
was in the heat of summer; and with his clothes
drenched with perspiration, as he tells us, he was
sent back in the evening to the Tower. Yet, weak
as his health had always been, he never succumbed.
Once or twice his voice and chest suffered, but he
notes himself, " I humbly thank God He so preserved my health that I never had so much as
half an hour's headache or other infirmity all
the time of this comfortless and tedious trial."
Tedious indeed it was; it fills 223 pages of the
folio "Troubles and Tryal." From the 12th of
March it dragged along, with occasional intervals,
till the end of July. Even Prynne was constrained
to admit the bravery of the old man's defence.

"To give him his due," he says, "he made as full,
as gallant, and as pithy defence of so bad a cause
as it was possible for the wit of man to invent, and
that with so much art, sophistry, vivacity, oratory,
audacity, and confidence, without the least blush
or acknowledgment of guilt in anything, as argued
him rather obstinate than innocent."

He goes on to hint that the bold and ingenious
character of the defence *proves* his allegiance to
the Church of Rome, as being more characteristic
of that Church than of the English.

Once only did the Archbishop's patience desert him. Mr. Nicolas, one of the chief prosecutors, took occasion to address him several times as the "pander to the whore of Babylon."

Laud said with great spirit that if such language was used to him again he would drop his defence ; he claimed at least to be treated as a Christian.

The Lords, aware that without a defence he would forfeit even the semblance of criminality, desired the speaker to confine himself to the evidence, and to have done with his rhetoric.

At last it became evident that there was not a single treasonous act, or even a trace of treasonable tendency in all the tenour of his life. Whereupon Serjeant Wilde said, with much legal acumen, that all the misdemeanours amounted to treason by a process of accumulation. "As if you were to say," said Hearne in the defence, "that two hundred black rabbits made one black horse." But it was a valuable phrase—treason by accumulation,—and on November 1st the Archbishop was ordered to the bar of the House of Commons. Here he spoke pathetically of "the slow hand, the heavy heart, and the old decayed memory," and condescended to plead.

On the 16th the Earl of Pembroke, Laud's successor in the Chancellorship of Oxford, made a violent speech in favour of the attainder in the House of Lords. The judges, when consulted, gave as their unanimous opinion that none of the charges proved against him amounted to treason by any known or established law.

On the 4th of January six Peers met and voted that he should suffer the punishment of a traitor. With some difficulty the Archbishop got the sentence of hanging commuted into beheading. The Commons ungraciously consented. It is curious that he should have been so anxious about it ; the death of a felon seemed to have offended his personal dignity—as a Peer he was privileged to decapitation.

When the tidings reached him that the attainder was passed, Laud's own manuscript breaks off.

Upon this the king sent him secretly from Oxford a full pardon, sealed with the Great Seal, which he received with very great joy, as a testimony of the king's continued affection.

CHAPTER XI

THE place where he suffered is probably more familiar to foreigners than to ourselves, though it is at our doors. Some of us may have visited the Tower in childhood—few of us visit it in later life.

The Tower abuts upon a great space now called Trinity Square, from the Trinity House which occupies the upper end of it. It is separated from it by the moat. The whole place is called Tower Hill. It is a low incline above the river. The view of the water and shipping is blocked by tall warehouses and wharves. Opposite the Tower is the Church of All-Hallows, Barking, a Gothic church spared by the fire of London, the interior quaintly fitted by Sir Christopher Wren. Its surname of Barking it owes to the fact that it was anciently a small dependency, technically a cell of the Abbey of Barking, in Essex. It is a living of which the Archbishop of Canterbury has long been patron. Laud was buried there first, before the body was transferred to Oxford.

The centre of the square is planted with trees and occupied by a quiet garden. The place where the scaffold stood is indicated by a dark pavement. On the Sunday when I first saw it, the whole place had a singularly peaceful, almost deserted look, as if it belonged to a past order of things, and had outlived the tragic memories and dismal scenes enacted within its limits. The air was pure and clear; there was no sound of traffic; it seemed to stand away even from the life of the mighty city that lay all about it. But all the week it is far different;—crowded with vehicles and thronged with passers-by, it lies at the very centre of the huge trading world. Here Laud suffered.

And here Heylyn rises into a strain so noble and so moving that I cannot forbear from giving the whole of his account : for, once read, it does not seem possible that any other should be written. It is of the very essence of high tragedy. There is no moralizing, no regret, no personal factor. A record in grave grand English of the words and deeds of the last great scene. About the whole of it there is no sadness, but a note of quiet triumph : the railing interruptions and pestering questions, the utter weariness of the sufferer and his intense desire to be gone ; and yet a magnificent collectedness, so that he is himself to

the last, with his quaint turns of expression and
characteristic mode of speech, till the busy life was
still. Whatever the life had been, it is one of the
great deaths of history.

"Meanwhile, the manner of his death troubled
the good Archbishop not a little; and with a
deeply Christian magnanimity and largeness of
heart, whatever some poor, unworthy minds have
thought or said about it, he was not above petition-
ing his malicious enemies, that, considering he was
a Bishop in the Church, he might die by beheading
rather than by the gibbet. Which request the
Commons at first violently refused, but did afterwards assent unto.

"The passing of the Ordinance being signified to
him by the then Lieutenant of the Tower, he
neither entertained the news with a stoical apathy,
nor wailed his fate with weak and womanish
lamentations (to which extremes most men are
carried in this case), but heard it with so even and
so smooth a temper, as shewed he neither was
ashamed to live, nor afraid to die. The time between the sentence and execution he spent in
prayers and supplications to the Lord his God;
having obtained, though not without some difficulty,
his chaplain, Dr. Sterne, who afterwards sat in the
Chair of York, to attend upon him. His chaplains,

Dr. Heywood and Dr. Martin, he much wished might be with him. But it seems it was too much for him to ask. So instead, two violent Presbyterians, Marshall and Palmer, were ordered by Parliament to give him religious consolations which consolations his Grace quietly declined. Indeed, little preparation was needed to receive that blow, which could not but be welcome, because long expected. For so well was he studied in the art of dying, especially in the last and strictest part of his imprisonment, that by continual fastings, watchings, prayers, and such like acts of Christian humiliation, his flesh was rarified into spirit, and the whole man so fitted for eternal glories, that he was more than half in heaven before death brought his bloody but triumphant chariot to convey him thither. He, that had so long been a Confessor, could not but think it a release of miseries to be made a Martyr.

" On the evening of the 9th, Sheriff Chambers, of London, brought the warrant for his execution. In preparation to so sad a work, he betook himself to his own, and desired also the prayers of others, and particularly of Dr. Holdsworth, fellow-prisoner in that place for a year and a half; though all that time there had not been the least converse betwixt them. This evening before his passover, the night

before the dismal combat betwixt him and death,
after he had refreshed his spirits with a moderate
supper, he betook himself unto his rest, and slept
very soundly till the time came in which his
servants were appointed to attend his rising. A
most assured sign of a soul prepared.

"The 10th of January came, on which the Archbishop completed his life of seventy-one years,
thirteen weeks, and four days. His death was the
more remarkable, in falling on St. William's day,
as if it did design him to an equal place in the
English Calendar with that which William, Archbishop of Bourges, had obtained in the French :
who (being as great a zealot in his time against
the spreading and increase of the Albigenses, as
Laud was thought to be against those of the
Puritan faction and the Scottish Covenanters) hath
ever since been honoured as a Saint and Confessor
in the Gallican Church ; the 10th of January being
destined for the solemnities of his commemoration,
on which day our Laud ascended from the scaffold
to a throne of glory.

"In the morning he was early at his prayers ; at
which he continued till Pennington, Lieutenant of
the Tower, and other public officers, came to conduct him to the scaffold ; which he ascended with
so brave a courage, such a cheerful countenance,

as if he had mounted rather to behold a triumph, than be made a sacrifice; and came not there to die, but to be translated. And though some rude and uncivil people reviled him, as he passed along, with opprobrious language, as loth to let him go to the grave in peace, yet it never discomposed his thoughts, nor disturbed his patience. For he had profited so well in the school of Christ, that 'when he was reviled, he reviled not again; when he suffered, he threatened not; but committed his cause to Him that judgeth righteously.'

"And, as he did not fear the frowns, so neither did he covet the applause of the people; and therefore rather chose to read what he had to speak, than to affect the ostentation either of memory or wit in that dreadful agony; whether with greater magnanimity than prudence can hardly be said. And here it followeth from the copy, presented very solemnly by Dr. Sterne to his sorrowing master, the good King Charles, at Oxford.

"THE ARCHBISHOP'S SPEECH UPON THE SCAFFOLD.

"'Good People, this is an uncomfortable time to preach; yet I shall begin with a text of Scripture, Hebrews xii. 2. "Let us run with patience the race which is set before us; looking unto Jesus,

the Author and Finisher of our faith, Who for the
joy that was set before Him endured the Cross,
despising the shame, and is set down at the right
hand of the throne of God."

"'I have been long in my race ; and how I have
looked unto Jesus, the Author and Finisher of my
faith, He best knows.   I am now come to the end
of my race, and here I find the Cross, a death of
shame.   But the shame must be despised, or no
coming to the right hand of God.   Jesus despised
the shame for me, and God forbid that I should
not despise the shame for Him.

"'I am going apace, as you see, towards the Red
Sea, and my feet are upon the very brink of it :
an argument, I hope, that God is bringing me into
the Land of Promise ; for that was the way through
which He led His people.

"'But before they came to it, He instituted a
passover for them.   A lamb it was ; but it must be
eaten with sour herbs.   I shall obey, and labour to
digest the sour herbs, as well as the lamb.   And
I shall remember it is the Lord's passover.   I shall
not think of the herbs, nor be angry with the hands
that gather them ; but look up only to Him who
instituted that, and governs these : for men can
have no more power over me than what is given
them from above.

"'I am not in love with this passage through the Red Sea, for I have the weakness and infirmity of flesh and blood plentifully in me. And I have prayed with my Saviour, *Ut transiret calix iste*, that this cup of red wine might pass from me. But if not, God's will, not mine, be done. And I shall most willingly drink of this cup as deep as He pleases, and enter into this sea, yea, and pass through it, in the way that He shall lead me.

"'But I would have it remembered, good people, that when God's servants were in this boisterous sea, and Aaron among them, the Egyptians which persecuted them, and did in a manner drive them into that sea, were drowned in the same waters, while they were in pursuit of them.

"'I know my God, Whom I serve, is as able to deliver me from this sea of blood, as He was to deliver the Three Children from the furnace. And (I most humbly thank my Saviour for it) my resolution is as theirs was: they would not worship the image which the king had set up, nor will I the imaginations which the people are setting up. Nor will I forsake the temple and the truth of God, to follow the bleating of Jeroboam's calves in Dan and in Bethel.

"'And as for this people, they are at this day miserably misled: God in His mercy open their eyes, that they may see the right way. For at this day the blind lead the blind; and if they go on, both will certainly fall into the ditch.

"'For myself, I am (and I acknowledge it in all humility) a most grievous sinner many ways—by thought, word, and deed; and yet I cannot doubt but that God hath mercy in store for me, a poor penitent, as well as for other sinners. I have now, upon this sad occasion, ransacked every corner of my heart; and yet I thank God I have not found among the many, any one sin which deserves death by any known law of this kingdom.

"'And yet hereby I charge nothing upon my judges: for if they proceed upon proof by valuable witnesses, I or any other innocent may be justly condemned. And I thank God, though the weight of the sentence lie heavy upon me, I am as quiet within as ever I was in my life.

"'And though I am not only the first Archbishop, but the first man, that ever died by an Ordinance in Parliament, yet some of my predecessors have gone this way, though not by this means: for Elphegus * was hurried away and lost his head by

* St. Elphegus or Alphege, as our Calendar calls him, was martyred for refusing to pay the precise sum at which the Danes assessed his ransom. The late Archdeacon Churton, to an unpublished paper of whose I have had access, vindicates Laud's right to the title of martyr on the ground that it has never been denied

the Danes; Simon Sudbury in the fury of Wat
Tyler and his fellows. Before these, St. John the
Baptist had his head danced off by a lewd woman;
and St. Cyprian, Archbishop of Carthage, submitted his head to a persecuting sword. Many
examples great and good ; and they teach me
patience. For I hope my cause in heaven will
look of another dye, than the colour that is put
upon it here.

"'And some comfort it is to me, not only that I
go the way of these great men in their several
generations, but also that my charge, as foul as it
is made, looks like that of the Jews against St.
Paul (Acts xxv. 8); for he was accused for the
law and the temple, *i.e.* religion ; and like that of
St. Stephen (Acts vi. 14) for breaking the ordinances which Moses gave, *i.e.* law and religion, the
holy place and the law (verse 13).

"'But you will say, Do I then compare myself
with the integrity of St. Paul and St. Stephen?
No : far be that from me. I only raise a comfort
to myself, that these great saints and servants of

to Alphege. He quotes a saying of Anselm on the same point.
" Nay," said Anselm, " Alphege died rather than he would allow
his dependants to be distressed by losing their property for him.
He who would rather lose his life than offend God by a small
offence, would much more certainly die than provoke Him by a
greater sin." The defence is ingenious, if a little sophistical.

God were laid at in their times, as I am now. And it is memorable that St. Paul, who helped on this accusation against St. Stephen, did after fall under the very same himself.

"'Yes, but here is a great clamour that I would have brought in Popery. I shall answer that more fully by and by. In the mean time, you know what the Pharisees laid against Christ Himself, 'If we let Him alone, all men will believe on Him, *et venient Romani,* and the Romans will come, and take away both our place and nation.' Here was a causeless cry against Christ, that the Romans would come: and see how just the judgment of God was. They crucified Christ for fear lest the Romans should come; and His death was it which brought in the Romans upon them, God punishing them with that which they most feared. And I pray God this clamour of *venient Romani* (of which I have given no cause) help not to bring them in. For the Pope never had such an harvest in England since the Reformation, as he hath now upon the sects and divisions that are amongst us. In the mean time, 'by honour and dishonour, by good report and evil report, as a deceiver and yet true,' am I passing through this world.

"'Some particulars also I think it not amiss to speak of.

"'1. And first, this I shall be bold to speak of the King, our gracious Sovereign. He hath been much traduced also for bringing in of Popery; but on my conscience (of which I shall give God a present account), I know him to be as free from this charge as any man living. And I hold him to be as sound a Protestant, according to the religion by law established, as any man in the kingdom; and that he will venture his life as far and as freely for it. And I think I do or should know both his affection to religion, and his grounds for it, as fully as any man in England.

"'2. The second particular is concerning this great and populous city (which God bless). Here hath been of late a fashion taken up to gather hands, and then go to the great court of the kingdom, the Parliament, and clamour for justice; as if that great and wise court, before whom the causes come which are unknown to the many, could not or would not do justice but at their appointment; a way which may endanger many an innocent man, and pluck his blood upon their own heads, and perhaps upon the city's also.

"'And this hath been lately practised against myself; the magistrates standing still, and suffering them openly to proceed from parish to parish without check. God forgive the setters of this; with

all my heart I beg it : but many well-meaning
people are caught by it.

"' In St. Stephen's case, when nothing else would
serve, they stirred up the people against him (Acts
vi. 12). And Herod went the same way : when
he had killed St. James, yet he would not venture
upon St. Peter, till he found how the other pleased
the people (Acts xii. 3).

"' But take heed of having your hands full of
blood (Isai. i. 15); for there is a time best known
to Himself, when God, above other sins, makes
inquisition for blood. And when that inquisition
is on foot, the Psalmist tells us that God remembers ; but that is not all : He remembers, and
forgets not the complaint of the poor, *i.e.* whose
blood is shed by oppression.

"' Take heed of this : " It is a fearful thing to fall
into the hands of the living God ;" but then especially when He is making inquisition for blood.
And with my prayers to avert it, I do heartily
desire this city to remember the prophecy that is
expressed in Jer. xxvi. 15.

"' 3. The third particular is, the poor Church of
England. It hath flourished, and been a shelter
to other neighbouring Churches, when storms have
driven upon them. But, alas! now it is in a storm
itself and God only knows whether or how it shall

get out. And, which is worse than a storm from without, it is become like an oak cleft to shivers with wedges made out of its own body; and at every cleft, profaneness and irreligion is entering in. While (as Prosper says) men that introduce profaneness are cloked over with the name *religionis imaginariæ,* of imaginary religion; for we have lost the substance, and dwell too much in opinion. And that Church, which all the Jesuits' machinations could not ruin, is fallen into danger by her own.

"'4. The last particular (for I am not willing to be too long) is myself. I was born and baptized in the bosom of the Church of England, established by law: in that profession I have ever since lived, and in that I come now to die.

"'What clamours and slanders I have endured for labouring to keep an uniformity in the external service of God, according to the doctrine and discipline of this Church, all men know, and I have abundantly felt. Now at last I am accused of high treason in Parliament, a crime which my soul ever abhorred. This treason was charged to consist of two parts—an endeavour to subvert the laws of the land; and a like endeavour to overthrow the true Protestant religion, established by law.

"'Besides my answers to the several charges, I

protested mine innocency in both Houses. It was said, Prisoners' protestations at the bar must not be taken. I must, therefore, come now to it upon my death, being instantly to give God an account for the truth of it.

"'I do therefore here, in the presence of God and His holy Angels, take it upon my death, that I never endeavoured the subversion either of law or religion. And I desire you all to remember this protest of mine for my innocency in this, and from all treasons whatsoever.

"'I have been accused likewise as an enemy of Parliaments. No; I understand them, and the benefit that comes by them, too well to be so. But I did dislike the misgovernments of some Parliaments many ways, and I had good reason for it; for *corruptio optimi est pessima.* And that being the highest court, over which no other hath jurisdiction, when it is misinformed or misgoverned, the subject is left without all remedy.

"'But I have done. I forgive all the world, all and every of those bitter enemies which have persecuted me; and humbly desire to be forgiven of God first, and then of every man. And so I heartily desire you to join in prayer with me.

"'O eternal God and merciful Father, look down upon me in mercy, in the riches and fulness of all

Thy mercies. Look upon me, but not till Thou hast nailed my sins to the Cross of Christ, not till Thou hast bathed me in the blood of Christ, not till I have hid myself in the wounds of Christ; that so the punishment due unto my sins may pass over me. And since Thou art pleased to try me to the uttermost, I most humbly beseech Thee, give me now, in this great instant, full patience, proportionable comfort, and a heart ready to die for Thine honour, the King's happiness, and this Church's preservation. And my zeal to these (far from arrogancy be it spoken) is all the sin (human frailty excepted, and all incidents thereto) which is yet known to me in this particular, for which I come now to suffer; I say, in this particular of treason. But otherwise, my sins are many and great. Lord, pardon them all, and those especially (whatever they are) which have drawn down this present judgment upon me. And when Thou hast given me strength to bear it, do with me as seems best in Thine own eyes. Amen.

"'And that there may be a stop of this issue of blood in this more than miserable kingdom, O Lord, I beseech Thee give grace of repentance to all blood-thirsty people. But if they will not repent, O Lord, confound all their devices, defeat and frustrate all their designs and endeavours upon them, which are or shall be contrary to the glory of Thy great Name, the truth and sincerity of religion, the establishment of the King, and his posterity after him, in their just rights and privileges ; the honour and conservation of Parliaments in their just power ; the preservation of this poor Church in her truth, peace, and patrimony; and the settlement of this distracted and distressed people, under their ancient laws, and in their native liberties.   And when Thou hast done all this in mere mercy for them, O Lord, fill their hearts with thankfulness, and with religious dutiful obedience to Thee and Thy commandments all their days. So, Amen, Lord Jesu, amen.   And receive my soul into Thy bosom.   Amen.

"'Our Father, which art in heaven, Hallowed be Thy Name. Thy kingdom come. Thy will be done in earth, As it is in heaven. Give us this day our daily bread. And forgive us our trespasses, As we forgive them that trespass against us. And lead us not into temptation ; But deliver us from evil : For Thine is the kingdom, and the power, and the glory, For ever and ever. Amen.'

"After these devotions, the Martyr rose, and gave his papers to Dr. Sterne, his chaplain, who went with him to his martyrdom, saying, 'Doctor, I give you this, that you may shew it to your fellow-chaplains, that they may see how I went out of the world ; and God's blessing and mercy be upon you and them.' Then turning to a person named Hinde, whom he perceived busy writing the words of his address, he said, ' Friend, I beseech you, hear me. I cannot say I have spoken every word as it is in my paper, but I have gone very near it, to help my memory as well as I could ; but I beseech you, let me have no wrong done me :' intimating that he ought not to publish an imperfect copy. 'Sir,' replied Hinde, 'you shall not. If I do so, let it fall upon my own head. I pray God have mercy upon your soul.' 'I thank you,' answered the holy Martyr ; 'I did not speak with any jealousy as if you would do so, but only, as a poor man going out of the world, it is not possible for me to keep to the words of my paper, and a phrase might do me wrong.'

"This said, he next applied himself to the fatal block, as to the haven of his rest. But finding the way full of people, who had placed themselves upon the theatre to behold the tragedy, he said, 'I thought there would have been an empty scaffold, that I might have had room to die. I beseech you, let me have an end of this misery, for I have endured it long.' Hereupon room was made for him to die. While he was preparing himself for the axe, he said, 'I will put off my doublets, and God's will be done. I am willing to go out of the world; no man can be more willing to send me out, than I am willing to be gone.'

"But there were broad chinks between the boards of the scaffold; and he saw that some people were got under the very place where the block was seated. So he desired either that the people might be removed, or dust brought to fill up the crevices, 'Lest,' said he, 'my innocent blood should fall upon the heads of the people.'

"The holy Martyr was now ready for death, and very calmly waiting for his crown. It was like a scene out of primitive times. His face was fresh and ruddy, and of a cheerful countenance. But there stood, to look on and rail, one Sir John Clotworthy, an Irishman, and follower of the Earl of Warwick. He was a violent and wrong-headed man, an enthusiast, and very furious as a demagogue. Being irritated that the revilings of the people moved not the strong quiet of the holy Martyr, or sharpened him into any show of passion, he would needs put in and try what he could do with his sponge and vinegar. So he propounded questions to him, not as if to learn, but rudely and out of ill nature, and to expose him to his associates. 'What,' asked he, 'is the comfortablest saying which a dying man would have in his mouth?' To which the holy Martyr with very much meekness answered, '*Cupio dissolvi et esse cum Christo.*' 'That is a good desire,' said the other; 'but there must be a foundation for that divine assurance.' 'No man can express it,' replied the Martyr; 'it is to be found within.' The busy man still pursued him, and said, ' It is founded upon a word, nevertheless, and that word should be known.' 'That word,' said the Martyr, 'is the knowledge of Jesus Christ, and that alone.' But he saw that this was but an indecent interruption, and that there would be no end to the trouble, and so he turned away from him to the executioner, as the gentler and discreeter person; and, putting some money into his hand, without the least distemper or change of countenance, he said, ' Here, honest friend, God forgive thee, and do thine office upon me in mercy.' Then did he go upon his knees, and the executioner said that he should give a sign for the blow to come; to which he answered, ' I will, but first let me fit myself.' After that he prayed.

"THE ARCHBISHOP'S PRAYER AS HE KNEELED BY THE BLOCK.

"'Lord, I am coming as fast as I can. I know I must pass through the shadow of death, before I can come to see Thee. But it is but *umbra mortis*, a mere shadow of death, a little darkness upon nature: but Thou by Thy merits and passions hast broke through the jaws of death. So, Lord, receive my soul, and have mercy upon me; and bless this kingdom with peace and plenty, and with brotherly love and charity, that there may not be this effusion of Christian blood amongst them, for Jesus Christ His sake, if it be Thy will.'

"Then he bowed his head upon the block, and prayed silently awhile. No man heard what it was he prayed in that last prayer. After that he said out loud, 'Lord, receive my soul,' which was the sign to the executioner, and at one blow he was beheaded.

"There was no malice which was too great for his miserable enemies. They said he had purposely painted his face, to fortify his cheeks against discovery of fear in the paleness of his complexion. But, as if for the confutation of this poor malice, his face, ruddy in the last moment, instantly after the blow turned white as ashes.

"Multitudes of people went with his body to the grave, which was borne in a leaden coffin to the church of All Hallows, Barking, a church of his own patronage and jurisdiction. It was noted of many as extraordinary, that, although the Liturgy had been by human law abolished, he, the great champion of the Church and her Ceremonies, was buried by his brave friends according to the old ritual, which it was high treason to use. So that it went to its grave with him. Both only for a while.

"'For my faith,' saith the holy Martyr, in his last Will and Testament, 'I die as I have lived, in the true orthodox profession of the Catholic Faith of Christ, foreshewed by the Prophets, and preached to the world by Christ Himself, His blessed Apostles, and their successors; and a true member of His Catholic Church, within the Communion of a living part thereof, the present Church of England, as it stands established by law.

"'I leave my body to the earth, whence it was taken, in full assurance of the resurrection of it from the grave at the last day. This resurrection I constantly believe my dear Saviour Jesus Christ will make happy unto me, His poor and weary servant. And for my burial, though I stand not much upon the place, yet if it conveniently may be, I desire to be buried in the Chapel of St. John

Baptist's College in Oxford, underneath the Altar
or Communion Table there.   And should I be so
unhappy as to die a prisoner, yet my earnest desire
is, I may not be buried in the Tower.   But where-
soever my burial shall be, I will have it private,
that it may not waste any of the poor means which
I leave behind me to better uses.'

"So, on the 24th of July, being St. James's Eve,
1663, the remains of the holy Martyr were translated to Oxford, and laid in one of the four brick
vaults beneath the Altar of St. John's.   And he
has no monument, except his own city of Oxford,
and the present English Church.

"'So the dead which he slew at his death were
more than they which he slew in his life.'"

NOTE.—The entry of Laud's burial in the register of All-Hallows
Church is interesting ; after his name, a word has been written and
erased by a later hand.   This word is either "traitor" or "martyr ; "
it is almost impossible to decide which.   Laud's nephew, Layfield,
was then rector of the church.

CHAPTER XII.

IN the personal appearance of the Archbishop there was little that was stately or commanding. His only dignity was gained from the sensation of restless energy that he inspired ; he was impressive because he knew his own mind, and had none of that uncertainty of speech and motion which are so fatal to true dignity. He was of almost diminutive mould, his face plump and rosy, but his frame if anything attenuated—he himself tells us this. The Little Vermin, the Urchin, the Little Great Man, Little Hocus Pocus are some of the names given him in treasonous correspondence. Of quick gestures and impetuous eager motions, he was restless and paced about as he thought or talked : more than once he strained and broke sinews in his legs from his fondness for this habit, and the hasty jerks he made in turning. He wore his hair cut very close, most unlike the court fashion of the day, though he retained the tiny moustache and imperial; and he affected a very plain dress, the rochet, scarf, and square cap in which he is painted, in great contrast to the gorgeous robes which the Primate of all England was able and had been accustomed to assume. It must be remembered that the idea of Bishops' *robes*, the lawn sleeves and satin chimere being assumed for public ceremonies and then laid aside, is a comparatively modern one. They are not even sacerdotal, or appropriate to consecrated buildings in any sense; that the Bishops wear their rochets in the House of Lords is a proof of this. A Roman Cardinal now often wears a cotta or short surplice over his scarlet.

The linen rochet, then,—a garment like a short surplice with small sleeves gathered in at the wrist, worn over a cassock,—and a scarf worn over the rochet, was Laud's ordinary dress: in this he dined, walked and went to Court, perhaps laying it aside in his own study, or when taking the little recreation which he thought it necessary to take.

He encouraged very rigorously plainness of dress among the clergy. One of the few rebukes recorded as having been addressed to him which he received with patience was on this subject. As Bishop of London he was holding a visitation in Essex, and took occasion publicly to reprove a clergyman whose dress seemed to him too magnificent and expensive, bidding him compare it with the plain habit which he was himself contented with. "My Lord," was the ready answer, "you have better clothes at home, and I have worse."

At Lambeth, the day began early; the Archbishop rose often before light, and spent an hour or more in prayer and quiet reading. Then his chaplains and secretaries went to him, and he had a simple breakfast of bread and water. Ale was usually drunk at this time. Enslaved as we are to tea, this is peculiarly repugnant to our notions; we value clear-headedness particularly in the early hours of the day: but, perhaps, by use, intoxicating liquors made no perceptible difference. Laud, however, eschewed ale, his tastes being simple, even ascetic, in the matter of food.

At about ten came the chapel service, attended by the household, consisting of over a hundred persons, all men. After this, dinner in the hall—a meal of somewhat indiscriminate hospitality, members of the Court being often present—the Archbishop and the more dignified guests sitting at the cross-table, which ran parallel to the upper end of the room. After this, he went to the Council in his barge, attended by his pikebearers, the pikes being still preserved at Lambeth; gave audiences or had

private interviews, generally in garden or gallery,
pacing about for the sake of the exercise ; then, at
four or five, evensong in the chapel, more study, and
bed after a light supper which he took in private.
It was a mere collegiate life, all in public, no
domesticity about it.   Even at Croydon, the country
seat, where his palace, long disused and given up to
baser uses, still exists, it was just the same.   It is
strangely unlike the modern episcopal life, where
the quiet household so invariably exists, with all
its rest and sympathy.   Here the only solitude
was the solitude of a crowd ; griefs and troubles
had to be carried alone ; triumphs received no
private impress of joy.

The only trace of recreation that we find in
Laud's life is to be discerned in his love of music.
That he should have put an organ into all the
houses he inhabited is, with his liturgical views, not
surprising; but his will speaks of " a harp, a chest
of viols, and a harpsico in his parlour at Lambeth," on which, perhaps, Orlando Gibbons, organist
of Westminster,* and reckoned " the sweetest finger
of the age," may have played.

On the whole we may say, though it has not been
the fashion to say so, that he was a humane man,
tender to poverty and distress.   Those who read the

---

* Laud was for some years a prebendary.

sentences of the Star Chamber, which it fell to
him as President to pronounce, will be inclined to
doubt this ; but we must remember that the shear-
ing away of ears was in the style of the time, and
did not seem to be any violation of the principles
of humanity. In fact, when Prynne was sentenced
to solitary confinement without books or writing
materials, he interfered : " Nay," he said, " I have
never known what it is to lack books and papers."

Again, he said to his chaplain, when Dr. Osbaldi-
stone, Master of Westminster School, was condemned to lose his ears for heresy, " I would go
down on my knees before the king to prevent the
execution of this cruel punishment." This is not
the speech of an inhuman man.

Once, indeed, in a moment of petulance, he acted
unworthily—he struck the weak. Archie Armstrong,
the last Court fool, a crack-brained jester gifted
with that shrewd clearness of thought that deficient
wits seem not unfrequently to confer, crossed his
path ; he indulged in that licence of mocking
speech conceded to his position.

The attempt to force the Liturgy on the Scotch
had just broken down, and the news arrived on the
11th of March. His Grace was going in to the
Council at Whitehall—in considerable irritation, no
doubt, at his favourite project having been so tur-

bulently shattered, even when backed by royal
authority. Archie met him in a passage of the
palace. " News from Scotland, your Grace," he said.
"Who's the fool now ? " This was too much for
Laud's patience. He went in and made a formal
complaint to the Council, and poor Archie was
condemned to lose his motley and be banished
from Court. It is rather like crushing a fly.
Archie's only *raison d'être* was his liberty to sting.

Laud was very impatient in his manner ; hated to
think that he was wasting time ; forgetting sometimes that he was perhaps serving his Church best
and doing his rank more credit by giving slow and
simple persons a patient hearing, though conscious
of a thousand other things of importance pressing
upon him, than by cutting them short, as he did
the poor gentleman from Wiltshire, mentioned
below, thus alienating the very class from which
the Church has always drawn her staunchest supporters — the honest slow-headed gentlemen, of
strong but not enthusiastic principles, the backbone
of the country.

This is well illustrated by the following episode.
The future Lord Clarendon, then Edward Hyde, a
young and rising barrister, was one of Laud's *pro-
tégés*, and owed practically everything to him. He
came to the conclusion that Laud was increasing

his unpopularity in the country and damaging
himself very seriously, even with the well-disposed,
by certain tricks of manner, or rather of bearing
and behaviour, by an abruptness of speech, by a
want of restraint in language, and by a general
disregard of those amenities of courtesy that are
worth so little in themselves, but so much to men
of high position, whose refusals should never be
ungracious, and whose rebukes should be administered with a gentle dignity and be obviously free
from all suspicion of personal animosity.

Mr. Hyde came to the conclusion that his Grace
had no one to tell him this, and that he could not
probably make a better return for all he owed to
Laud than by being perfectly candid and open
with him.

Professor Mozley, by representing Hyde as con-
sequential and officious, has obscured, I think, the
true spirit of the interview. He represents Hyde
as finding it a congenial and delightful task, and
entering upon it with feelings of solemn happiness, as one who had a high and gracious duty to
perform. But I think it is clear that he shrank
very much from the task, and only went through
with it from a feeling of strict duty : though there is
a touch of natural complacency about the record,
it is rarely a pleasant thing to tell a man an un-

pleasant truth about himself. There are some
natural pedagogues and self-made dominies in the
world—but not among the young ; and surely a
successful young man like Hyde is very unlikely
to have been already censorious. When, too, we
reflect that the individual to be enlightened was
his guide, philosopher, and friend, the benefactor to
whom he owed everything, we need not hesitate to
decide that it was a disagreeable duty, the kind of
duty of which a man thinks with strong distaste
when he wakes in the morning of the appointed day.

He went early to Lambeth, and found that the
Archbishop was getting a little walk in the garden.
He was received very kindly, as he always was ;
invited to take a turn with him. " What good
news from the country, Mr. Hyde ? " said his Grace,
unconsciously giving him a chance.

Mr. Hyde answered that there was none good :
the people were universally discontented, and (which
troubled him most) that many people spoke extreme
ill of his Grace, as the cause of all that was amiss.

The Archbishop replied that he was sorry for it ;
he knew he did not deserve it ; and that he must
not give over serving the king and Church to please
the people.

Mr. Hyde told him he thought he need not lessen
his zeal for either, and that it grieved him to find

people of the best conditions, who loved both king
and Church, exceedingly undevoted, complaining
of his manner of treating them when they had
occasion to resort to him,—and then named two
persons of most interest and credit in Wiltshire,
who had that summer attended the council board ;
adding that all the Lords present used them with
great courtesy, and that he alone spake sharply to
them ; and one of them, supposing that somebody
had done him ill offices, and spoken slanderously of
him to his Grace, went the next morning to Lambeth
to present his service to him, and to discover, if he
could, what misrepresentation had been made of
him ; that, after he had attended very long, he was
admitted to speak with his Grace, who, scarce hearing him, sharply answered him that " *he had no time
for compliments,*" which put the other much out of
countenance : and that this kind of behaviour was
the discourse of companies of all persons of quality.

The Archbishop heard the relation very patiently
and attentively, and discoursed over every particular
with all imaginable condescension, and said, with
evident show of trouble, that he was very unfortunate to be so ill understood ; that he meant very
well ; that by an imperfection of nature, which, he
said, often troubled him, he might deliver the resolution of the Council in such a tone and with a

sharpness of voice that made men believe he was angry when he was no such thing.

That he did well remember that one of them (who was a person of honour) came afterwards to him, at a time when he was shut up about an affair of importance which required his full thoughts; but that, as soon as he heard of the other's being without, he sent for him, himself going into the next room, and received him very kindly, as he thought; and supposing he came about business, asked him what the business was; and the other, answering that he had no business, but continuing his address with some ceremony, he had indeed said that he had no time for compliments, but he did not think he went out of the room in that manner.

He added that he was pleased with Mr. Hyde for speaking frankly, and would be glad to hear anything which he had to say.

Whereupon Mr. Hyde observed that the gentlemen had too much reason for the report they made, and he did not wonder they had been much troubled with his carriage toward them; that he did exceedingly wish he would more reserve his passion, and would treat persons of quality and honour and interest in the country with more courtesy and condescension.

His Grace said, smiling, that he could only undertake for his heart—that he meant very well; as for
his tongue, he could not undertake not sometimes
to speak more heartily and sharply than he should
do (which oftentimes he was sorry and reprehended
himself for), and in a tone which might be liable to
misinterpretation with them which were not well
acquainted with him.

After this free discourse, Mr. Hyde ever found
himself more graciously received by him, and treated
with more familiarity, from which he concluded
that if the Archbishop had had any true friend
who could in proper seasons have dealt frankly
with him, he would not only have received it very
well, but have profited by it.

Laud was wise enough not to undervalue this
plain speech, so difficult for persons in high authority, especially when they are not of at all a confidential nature, to get at,—and great enough, too, to
feel no sort of resentment against the teller of
home truths : it is so common in such cases to profit
by the advice, and not to forgive the adviser.

Personally, it must be remembered, Laud was a
very shy man ; he had evidently few really genial
impulses. It was not his idea of happiness to be
surrounded by cheerful acquaintances ; he had not
the true instinct for hospitality, so important a

qualification for a Bishop from the earliest times.
The union of a business-like liturgical temperament
with this shyness is not uncommon ; and his brisk,
authoritative manner was, as it so often is, a refuge
from the feeling of personal uneasiness in the
presence of strangers.

His extreme, almost morbid, sensibility to libels
and hostile public demonstrations is very remarkable.   I have had occasion to allude to it incidentally more than once ; but the following pathetic
interview with Heylyn, never, I think, before quoted,
is a good instance of this, besides being, to my
mind, the best testimony to his absolute sincerity
of feeling with regard to the Church of Rome that
we possess.

"In the November of this year (1639) I received
a message from him to attend him the next day,
at two o'clock in the Afternoon.   The key being
turned which opened the way into his Study, I
found him sitting in a Chair, holding a paper in
both hands, and his eyes so fixed upon the Paper
that he observed me not at my coming in.   Finding
him in that Posture, I thought it fit in manners to
retire again ; but the noise I made by my retreat
bringing him back unto himself, he recalled me to
him, and told me, after some short pause, that
he well remembered he had sent for me, but could

not tell for his life what it was about. After which he was pleased to say (not without tears in his eyes) that he had then newly received a letter acquainting him with the revolt of a person of quality in N. Wales to the Church of Rome: that he knew the increase of Popery by such frequent revolts would be imputed unto him and his brethren Bishops, who were least guilty of the same: that for his part he had done his utmost, so far as it might consist with the Rules of Prudence and the preservation of the Church, to suppress that party and to bring the chief sticklers in it to condign punishment. To the truth whereof (lifting up his wet eyes to Heaven) he took God to witness: conjuring me (as I would answer it to God at the Day of Judgement) that if ever I should come to any of those places which he and his Brethren by reason of their great age were not likely to hold long, I would employ all such abilities as God had given me, in suppressing the Romish party, who by their open undertakings and secret practices were like to be the ruin of this flourishing Church."

If further testimony is required, subjoined is a celebrated letter of Laud's to Sir Kenelm Digby, on the conversion of the latter to Roman Catholicism.

Sir Kenelm Digby, eldest son of Sir Everard Digby who suffered for his share in the Gunpowder

Plot, was a man who once enjoyed the reputation
of a philosopher. He certainly took the fancy of
the time, and was, for a little, one of the best-
known men in England.

His exact connection in early life with Laud is
not easy to discover, but it is stated that he was
brought up under Laud's direction, when Dean
of Gloucester. This would mean, educated in his
house, and thus might stand for a very close,
almost paternal relation.

He first came before the world as the inventor
or rather propagator of an astounding medical
fiction, named " Sympathetic Powder," by which
wounds were to be healed in the absence of the
patient. Perhaps, according to modern lights,
this kind of healing is not so incredible as would
appear.

He got a reputation by his gallant conduct at
the siege of Algiers, in 1628, where he seems to
have fought like a Viking ; and in 1636 he excited
a very general interest by becoming a convert
to the Church of Rome. The letter subjoined,
which is interesting both on public and private
grounds, was written by Laud on this occasion.

He was a prisoner under the Commonwealth
and was cited as a witness in Laud's trial, on the
subject of the offer of the Cardinal's hat, when he

stated his firm belief in Laud's staunch Protestantism. He was set at liberty by the special request
of the Court of France, and transferred himself to
that country, where he met Descartes, and in
collaboration with him produced some curious
philosophical treatises. He died in 1665.

His handsome presence and great powers of
conversation, or rather monologue, seem to have
made him a celebrity, and his life certainly com-
bines the elements of romantic interest in the
highest degree.

ARCHBISHOP LAUD'S LETTER TO SIR
KENELM DIGBY.

" Salutem in Christo.

" WORTHY SIR,

"I am sorry for all the contents of your
Letter, save that which expresses your love to me.
And I was not a little troubled at the very first
words of it. For you begin, that my Lord
Ambassador told you I was not pleased to hear
you had made a defection from the Church of
England. It is most true, I was informed so ; and
thereupon I writ to my Lord Ambassador, to know
what he heard of it there. But it is true likewise,
that I writ to yourself ; and Mr. Secretary Cook

sent my Letters very carefully. Now seeing your Letters mentioned my Lord Ambassador's speech with you, without any notice taken of my writing; I could not but fear these Letters of mine came not to your hands. Out of this fear, your second Letters took me; for they acknowledged the receipt of mine, and your kind acceptance of them. Had they miscarried, I should have held it a great misfortune. For you must needs have condemned me deeply in your own thoughts, if in such a near and tender business, I should have solicited my Lord Ambassador, and not written to yourself.

"In the next place I thank you, and take it for a great testimony of your love to me, that you have been pleased to give me so open and clear account of your proceedings with yourself in this matter of religion. In which, as I cannot but commend the strict reckoning, to which you have called yourself; so I could have wished, before you had absolutely settled the foot of that account, you would have called in some friend, and made use of his eyes as a bye-stander, who oftentimes sees more than he that plays the game. You write, I confess, that after you had fallen upon these troublesome thoughts, you were nigh two years in the diligent discussion of this matter; and that you omitted no industry, either of conversing with learned men, or of reading the best authors, to beget in you a right intelligence of this subject. I believe all this, and you did wisely to do it. But I have some questions, out of the freedom of a friend, to ask about it. Were not all the learned men, you conversed with for this particular, of the Roman party? Were not the best authors, you mention, of the same side? If both men and authors were the same way, can they beget any righter intelligence in you, than is in themselves? If they were men and authors on both sides, with whom you conversed; why was I (whom you are pleased to style one of your best friends) omitted? True, it may be, you could not reckon me among those learned men and able for direction, with whom you conversed : suppose that; yet yourself accounts me among your friends. And is it not many times as useful, when thoughts are distracted, to make use of the freedom and openness of a friend not altogether ignorant, as of those which are thought more learned, but not so free, nor perhaps so indifferent?

"But the result, you say, that first began to settle you, was, that you discerned by this your diligent conversation, and studious reading, that there were great mistakings on both sides, and that passion and affection to a party transported

too many of those that entered into the lists in
this quarrel. Suppose this also to be true, I am
heartily sorry, and have been ever since I was of
any understanding in matters of religion, to hear
of sides in the Church. And I make no doubt,
but it will one day fall heavy upon all that wilfully
make, or purposely continue, sidings in that body.
But when sides are made and continued, remember
you confess there are great mistakings on both
sides. And how, then, can you go from one side
to the other, but you must go from one great mistaking to another? And if so, then by changing
the side, you do but change the mistaking, not
quit yourself from mistakes. And if you do quit
yourself from them, by God's goodness, and your
own strength ; yet why might not that have been
done without changing the side, since mistakes are
on both sides? As for the passion and transpor-
tation of many that enter the lists of this quarrel,
I am sure you mean not to make their passion
your guide ; for that would make you mistake
indeed. And why, then, should their passion work
upon your judgment? especially, since the passion
as well as the mistakes are confessed to be on both
sides.

"After this follows the main part of your Letters,
and that which principally resolved you to enter

again the communion of the Church of Rome, in which you had been born and bred, against that semblance of good reason, which formerly had made you adhere to the Church of England.

"And first you say, you now perceive that you may preserve yourself in that Church, without having your belief bound up in several particulars, the dislike whereof had been a motive to you to free yourself from the jurisdiction which you conceived did impose them. It is true all Churches have some particulars free. But doth that Church leave you free to believe, or not believe, any thing determined in it? And did not your former dislike arise from some things determined in and by that Church? And if so, what freedom see you now, that you saw not then? And you cannot well say that your dislike arose from any thing not determined; for in those, the jurisdiction of that Church imposes not.

"You add, that your greatest difficulties were solved, when you could distinguish between the opinions of some new men raised upon some wrested inferences, and the plain and solid articles of faith delivered at the first. Why, but I cannot but be confident you could distinguish these long since, and long before you joined yourself to the Church of England. And that therefore your

greatest difficulties (if these were they) were as
fully and fairly solved then, as now they are, or
can be. Besides, if by these plain and solid Articles
you mean none but the Creed (and certainly no
other were delivered at the first), you seem to intimate by comparing this and the former passage,
that so you believe these plain and first Articles,
you may preserve yourself in that Church, from
having your belief bound up to other particulars ;
which I think few will believe, besides yourself, if
you can believe it. And the opinions of new men,
and the wrested inferences upon these, are some
of those great mistakes which you say are on both
sides, and therefore needed not to have caused
your change.

"To these first Articles you say, The Church in
no succeeding age hath power to add (as such) the
least tittle of new doctrine. Be it so ; and I believe it heartily (not as such), especially if you
mean the Articles of the Creed. But yet if that
Church do maintain, that all her decisions in a
General Council, are Articles *Fidei Catholicæ*, and
that all Christians are bound to believe all and
every one of them, *cadem Fide, qua Fidei Articulos ;*
and that he is an heretic which believes them not
all ; where is then your freedom, or your not being
bound up in several particulars ? And if you reply,

you dislike no determination which that Church hath made ; then why did you formerly leave it, to free yourself from that jurisdiction that you conceived imposed them? For if the things which troubled you were particulars not determined, they were not imposed upon your belief. And if they were determined, and so imposed, how are you now set free more than then ?

"You say again, You see now, that to be a Catholic, doth not deprive them of the forenamed liberty, who have abilities to examine the things you formerly stuck at, and drive them up to their first principles. But first then ; what shall become of their liberty, who are not able to examine? shall they enthral their consciences ? Next, what shall secure them, who think themselves, and are perhaps thought by others, able to examine, yet indeed are not ? Thirdly ; what assurance is there in cases not demonstrable (as few things in religion are), that they which are able to examine, have either no affection to blind their judgment, or may not mistake themselves and their way in driving a doubtful point to its first principles ? Lastly ; how much doth this differ from leaning upon a private spirit, so much cried out against by that side, when men, under pretence of their ability, shall examine the tenets of the Church, and assume a

N

liberty to themselves under colour of not being bound ?

" But, you say, this is not the breaking of any obligation that the Church lays upon you ; but only an exact understanding of the just and utmost obligations that side ties men to. I must here question again. For, first, what shall become of their freedom, that cannot reach to this exact understanding ? And next, do not you make yourself, as a private man, judge of the Church's obligations upon you ? And is it not as great an usurpation upon the Church's power and right, to be judge of her obligations, as of her tenets ? For if the points be left free, there is no obligation ; nor can you, or need any other, have any scruple. But if the points be binding by the predetermination of the Church, can you any way be judge of her obligation, but you must be judge also of the point to which she obliges ? Now, I think, that the Church will hardly give liberty to any private man to be so far her judge, since she scarce allows so much to any, as *judicium discretionis,* in things determined by her.

" These utmost obligations, to which that side ties men, you believe many men (and not of the meanest note) pass over in gross, without ever thoroughly entering into the due consideration thereof. And truly I believe so too, that among too many men on both sides, neither the points nor the obligations to them are weighed as they ought. But that is no warrant (pardon my freedom) that yourself hath considered them in all circumstances, or that you have considered them better now than you did before, when the dislike of that imposing jurisdiction was your first motive to free yourself from it by joining to the Church of England.

"And whereas you say, that you have returned into that Communion, who from your birth had right of possession in you, and therefore ought to continue it, unless clear and evident proof (which you say surely cannot be found) should have evicted you from it : truly, Sir, I think this had been spoken with more advantage to you and your cause, before your adhering to the Church of England, than now ; for then right of possession could not have been thought little. But now, since you deserted that Communion, either you did it upon clear and evident proof, or upon apparent only. If you did it then upon clear and evident proof, why say you now no such can be found ? If you did it but upon apparent and seeming proof (a semblance of very good reason, as yourself calls it), why did you then come off from that Communion, till your proof were clear and evident ? And why may not that, which now seems clear and evident, be but apparent, as well as that, which then seemed clear unto you, be but semblance now? Nor would I have you say, that clear and evident proof cannot be found for a man, in this case of religion, to forego the Communion which had right of possession in him from his birth; for the proposition is an universal negative, and of hard proof. And therefore, though I think I know you and your judgment so well, that I may not without manifest wrong charge you, that you did in this great action, and so nearly concerning you, *ad pauca respicere,* which our great Master tells us breeds facile and easy, rather than safe and warrantable determinations, yet it will be upon you not only in honour without, but also in conscience within, to be able to assure yourself that you did *ad plurima,* if not *ad omnia respicere.*

"The thing being so weighty in itself, and the miserable division of Christendom (never sufficiently to be lamented) making the doubt so great, that you who have been on both sides, must needs be under the dispute of both sides, whether this last act of yours, be not in you rather a relapse into a former sickness, than a recovery from a former fall.

"But against this, the temper of your mind (you say) arms you against all censures, no slight air of

reputation being able to move you. In this, I must
needs say, you are happy; for he that can be
moved from himself by the changeable breath of
men, lives more out of than in himself; and (which
is a misery beyond all expression) must in all
doubts go to other men for resolution; not to himself; as if he had no soul within him. But yet *post
conscientiam fama.* And though I would not desire
to live by reputation; yet would I leave no good
means untried, rather than live without it. And
how far you have brought yourself in question,
which of these two, conscience or reputation, you
have shaken by this double change, I leave yourself to judge; because you say your first was with
a semblance of very good reason. And though
you say again, that it now appears you were then
misled; yet you will have much ado to make the
world think so.

"The way you took in concealing this your
resolution of returning into that Communion, and
the reasons which you give why you so privately
carried it here, I cannot but approve. They are
full of all ingenuity, tender and civil respects, fitted
to avoid discontent in your friends, and scandal
that might be taken by others, or contumely that
might be returned upon yourself. And as are
these reasons, so is the whole frame of your Letter

(setting aside that I cannot concur in judgment)
full of discretion and temper, and so like yourself,
that I cannot but love even that which I dislike in
it.   And though I shall never be other than I have
been to the worth of Sir Kenelm Digby ; yet most
heartily sorry I am, that a man whose discourse did
so much content me, should thus slide away from me,
before I had so much as suspicion to awaken me, and
suggest that he was going.   Had you put me into a
dispensation, and communicated your thoughts to
me before they had grown up into resolutions, I am
a priest, and would have put on what secresy you
should have commanded.   A little knowledge I have
(God knows, a little), I would have ventured it with
you in that serious debate you have had with yourself.   I have ever honoured you, since I knew your
worth, and I would have done all offices of a friend
to keep you nearer than now you are.   But since
you are gone, and settled another way, before you
would let me know it, I know not now what to say
to a man of judgment ; and so resolved : for to
what end should I treat, when a resolution is set
already ?   So set, as that you say no clear and
evident proof can be found against it : nor can I
tell how to press such a man as you to ring the
changes in religion.   In your power it was not to
change ; in mine it is not to make you change

again. Therefore to the moderation of your own
heart, under the grace of God, I must and do now
leave you for matter of religion ; but retaining still
with me, and entirely, all the love and friendliness
which your worth won from me ; well knowing, that
all differences in opinion shake not the foundations
of religion.

"Now to your Postscript, and then I have done.
That I am the first and the only person to whom
you have written thus freely : I thank you heartily
for it. For I cannot conceive any thing thereby,
but your great respect to me, which hath abundantly spread itself all over your Letter. And had
you written this to me, with a restraint of making
it further known, I should have performed that
trust : but since you have submitted it to me, what
further knowledge of it I shall think fit to give to
any other person ; I have, as I took myself bound,
acquainted his Majesty with it, who gave a great
deal of very good expression concerning you, and
is not a little sorry to lose the service of so able a
subject. I have likewise made it known in private
to Mr. Secretary Cook, who was as confident of
you as myself. I could hardly believe your own
Letters, and he as hardly my relation. To my
Secretary I must needs trust it, having not time to
write it again out of my scribbled copy ; but I dare

trust the secresy in which I have bound him. To
others I am silent, and shall so continue, till the
thing open itself ; and I shall do it out of reasons,
very like to those which you give, why yourself
would not divulge it here. In the last place, you
promise yourself, that the condition you are in will
not hinder me from continuing to be the best friend
you have. To this I can say no more, than that
I could never arrogate myself to be your best
friend ; but a poor, yet respected friend of yours
I have been, ever since I knew you ; and it is not
your change, that can change me, who never yet
left, but where I was first forsaken ; and not always
there. So praying for God's blessing upon you,
and in that way which He knows most necessary
for you, I rest,

   " Your very loving friend,

    " To serve you in Domino,

      " W : CANT :

" LAMBETH, *March* 27, 1636.

" I have writ this Letter freely; I shall look upon
all the trust that ever you mean to carry with me,
that you shew it not, nor deliver any copy to any
man. Nor will I look for any answer to the queries
I have herein made. If they do you any good,
I am glad; if not, yet I have satisfied myself. But
leisure I have none, to write such Letters ; nor

will I entertain a quarrel in this wrangling age ; and now my strength is past. For all things of moment in this Letter, I have pregnant places in the Council of Trent, Thomas, Bellarmin, Stapleton, Valentia, etc. But I did not mean to make a volume of a Letter.

" Endorsed this with the Archbishop's own hand. March 27, 1636."

CHAPTER XIII

HIS preference in favour of a celibate clergy
was very strong. "*Ceteris paribus*," he once
said before the king at Woodstock, "he intended,
in the exercise of his patronage, to prefer the
single to the married." This statement was mis-
interpreted, but he dexterously contrived to avert
the virulence of the misrepresentation by presiding
a very short time after, at the marriage of a
chaplain of his, Thomas Turner, in the Chapel of
London House, to a daughter of Sir Francis
Windebank, afterwards Secretary of State upon
Laud's own recommendation. And to a certain
extent he was undoubtedly right. No doubt a
married clergy has preserved us from other evils
so great as to demand any sacrifice ; but, on the
other hand, it is certain that a man who is
bound not only to secure a living for himself
but a provision for his family out of the Church
revenues will not be likely, unless he has private

sources of income, to spend the revenues of the
Church in a single-hearted way. No one can
find fault with the ancient system of putting vast
sacred revenues into the hands of pious single
men. They were expected to be munificently
disposed of in a grand public way. It is only
necessary to refer to the names William of Wykeham, Waynflete, and innumerable others to be
assured of this; and great exception may justly
be taken to the placing of these great trusts into
the hands of family men. The huge fortunes
wrung out of the Church into private hands, so
characteristic of the last century, will have to be
atoned for some time, and Laud's position is by
no means an unreasonable one.

Everything at Lambeth was arranged on this
principle. No womankind were allowed in the
great establishment. And Laud himself seems
to have carried it still further—he had no friendship with women; he had no natural inclination for
feminine gentleness and the sweetness they add to
life. Mrs. Maxwell, wife of the Black Rod, in
whose house he was kept for nearly a year, con-
fided to her gossips that he was the most pious
soul she had ever seen, but that he was a silly
fellow to talk to a woman.

Curiously enough this custom was maintained

at Lambeth till a late date. The wife and family
of the Archbishop resided at a house outside the
palace, known as " Mrs. Moore's " or " Mrs. Manners
Sutton's lodging." In the time of the latter the
young ladies of the family were conducted there
by footmen with flambeaux every night, after
having paid a respectful adieu to their parent by
kissing his hand, and returned to breakfast in
the morning.

Laud had a bountiful mind. His munificence
was princely. He had no kind of taint of niggard-
liness or selfish saving in his composition. The
Church had lavished her worldly gifts upon him,
and he distributed them royally. It had invariably
been his custom when inducted into a living,—and
he had held many,—to set aside a fixed proportion
of the stipend as an annual pension for twelve
poor persons in the parish ; to reserve one-fifth for
charity ; to rebuild or repair the parsonage house.
Wherever he went, at Abergwili, at St. John's, at
Lambeth, at Reading, he built and restored screens
and windows, organs and sacred vessels. Upon
these he lavished wealth. He gave the University
of Oxford over a thousand manuscripts ; he en-
dowed the Arabic professorship there. The only
complaint of the kind made against him was by
the Kentish gentry and clergy, who complained

that the old diocesan entertainments had given place to a general hospitality. They contrasted him unfavourably with Abbot. "His servants," they said, "hung about Westminster Hall, St. Paul's, and the Royal Exchange, with tickets of invitation in their hands, to catch persons of quality"; this they grudged. He died a moderately wealthy man. His will is still extant—there are innumerable legacies to old servants and relations. He bequeaths seven magnificent rings. The following entries are worth noting :—

"I take the boldness to give to my Deare and Dread Sovereign King Charles (whom God blesse) 1,000*l.*, and I doe forgive him the Debt which hee owes me, being 2,000*l.*, and require that the two tallies for it be delivered up.

"I give to the R^t Honourable George, Ld Duke of Buckingham, his grace, my chalice and patens of Gold; and theis I desire the young Duke to accept and use in his Chapell, as the memorial of him who had a faithfull heart to love, and the honour to be beloved of his father. Soe God bless him with wise and good counsells, and a heart to follow them."

In his life he never fell into the least degree of nepotism, so common and so excusable a fault of the age. It was said that he relieved his friends,

but would not raise them. He had a near kins-
man, Fuller tells us, at Oxford, a good scholar, but
of a wild and indolent disposition, and inclined to
trust to his relationship with the great man. This
lad he utterly refused to help or advance till he
should altogether reform himself. "Breed up your
children well," he is recorded to have said to a
needy relative, "and I will do what I can and
ought to raise them."

As might have been expected, one of the pro-
jects into which he flung himself with the greatest
enthusiasm was the restoration of St. Paul's.

Old St. Paul's, one of the least respectable of
historical monuments, was a structure of immense
length and height, but ill-built and inconvenient
to the highest degree. It had an ugly wooden
vaulting throughout. The nave had become a kind
of Burlington Arcade ; it was lined with shops, and
was a fashionable promenade,—literally a "den
of thieves." It was a noted place for criminal
assignations. The whole edifice was leaky and
shaky, the foundations having subsided in the most
alarming manner. The vast spire had fallen down,
struck by lightning, and was replaced by a low
pediment.

King James took up the task, and contributed
a large sum. Inigo Jones was set to work, and

succeeded in producing one of the most horrible and incongruous enormities that have ever disgraced the earth. It was not even quaint.

The tower was adorned with four gigantic Ionic volutes in place of flying buttresses, and an Ionic portico was added at the west, together with such other additions as the growing classical taste suggested. Houses were pulled down about it, so as to afford a clear view of one of the most amazing of structures.

Laud, with a zeal for collecting that would have done credit to the nineteenth century, begged right and left; he got portions of the effects of intestate persons diverted to it. One story is worth quoting. A brewer near Lambeth had a chimney which vomited an offensive smoke over the gardens. One day when Laud was walking there with Noy, the Attorney-General, it was particularly noticeable. Noy offered to have it suppressed as a nuisance. Laud said that he preferred enduring the smoke to interfering with an honest man. When Noy was gone he sent for the brewer, told him what had occurred, adding that if he would atone for it by a gift of £20 to St. Paul's no more should be said. The man offered £10. Laud refused to bargain, and the law took its course; the chimney was condemned.

He was fond of talking to specialists, especially on Political or Economic questions, and astonished them by the depth and lucidity of his grasp of their subject and his extreme quickness at seizing points. His diligence, when Commissioner of the Treasury, in inquiring into the details of the Custom House, especially with regard to tobacco, was unfavourably commented upon by the Puritans.

"He might have spent his time," they said, "better, and more for his grace, in the Pulpit, than sharking and raking in the Tobacco shop."

Of the chief nobility and gentry he kept a secret catalogue, in which he entered notable facts, and analysed their dispositions and tendencies.

He had a high, harsh, and irritable voice—full of that kind of unconscious irritability that nervous energy and uneasy health are apt to give. His tendency to offend people unintentionally has been already alluded to, but his unconciliatory attitude shows itself, perhaps, most markedly in the extreme odium he incurred among the chief advisers of the Crown. Here and there came an uncompromising advocate of the antique loyalty, like Strafford, whose respect for the office carried him over the initial dislike to the man, and his sharp imperious manner, that so many felt. But, as a rule, they hated his bluntness and incorruptibility; they writhed beneath his cold just criticisms ; they felt no sort of enthusiasm for the cause which he served so devotedly. And, at the same time, he was a terrible antagonist ; his character was so impersonal, so independent, so pure, that it was ludicrous to allege double-dealing, self-interest, or slackness against him. They went a different way to work. Weston, the Lord Treasurer, fabricated untruths consistently, but Lord Cottington, Chancellor of the Exchequer, set to work on far more subtle lines.

The following incident will afford the best possible illustration of this. Charles, who inherited from his father a passionate love of hunting, determined, with that unreasonable tenacity that has seemed to some so regal an attribute, to construct a gigantic park, between Richmond and Hampton Court, for red and fallow-deer, and to have it walled in—the circuit being somewhat over ten miles—at national expense.

The time was not a happy one. The Exchequer was low ; the calls for money had been already far too vehement. To gratify a private whim at such a time was one of those unhappy mistakes which Charles was always committing. And his temper on these points was fatal ; he imagined it to be inconsistent with his dignity or his duty to make any concessions.

O

It was not merely walling-in of waste grounds; there were commons to be compensated for, farmers to be bribed, gentlemen to be bought out of lands held as freehold or on Crown leases. The king offered royal terms because he was utterly unable to afford it. Many yielded; some refused. One obstinate Naboth, with the largest estate of all, gave people in general to understand that tyranny was beginning in earnest; that private property was no longer safe from the rapacity of the Crown.

Lord Cottington received a number of petitions, and interviewed many complainants, and taking the whole business very much to heart, tried, by much importunity and all sorts of legal delays, to divert the king's purpose. At last Charles' sense of dignity took fire. He told Cottington, who had come for an audience, with a number of patent petty reasons, that he was resolved to go through with it, and had already caused "brick to be burned, and much of the wall to be built on his own land." Upon which Cottington gathered up his papers, and went, in much discontent and distress. He had honestly tried to serve the king in delaying this selfish and irritating project; and his interference was merely considered impertinent.

Before long this unpopular scheme of the king's became common talk. Laud made up his mind that he must remonstrate ; much as he disliked the process, and much as he disapproved of standing in opposition to the Anointed Sovereign, yet that the king should be dear in the hearts of his people was a stronger motive.

He spoke, and received an indifferent, indecisive answer ; he concluded, indeed, from it that the king's mind was made up, but that his resolution had been formed in consequence of insufficient information of the mischief it was causing. Whereupon he went to Cottington, having heard by rumour that he had made some opposition to it, and urgently, and with great warmth, pressed him to give the king good counsel in the matter.

Whether Cottington was seized with sudden irritation at the patronizing way in which this was done, and at the unwarrantable interference of the Archbishop, or whether it was part of a deep malevolent plan to bring Laud into discredit, is not certain. Whichever it was, it shows Laud's unhappy touch in dealing with official pride, and his inaptitude for delicate diplomacy. At all events Cottington, in his gravest manner, stated that in his opinion the king's wishes were perfectly reasonable, as the place was so convenient for his winter exercise, that no one who wished him to be well could conscientiously dissuade him.

Whereupon Laud took fire. Ugly words came from him. He spoke of ruin and false counsellors, alienation of subjects from their king, and the doom of treachery. Cottington, delighted to see the conflagration flourish, proceeded to say that to dissuade the king from his project could only proceed from a want of affection to his person,—was not sure, indeed, that it could not be called treason. Laud, too angry to see through this solemn but transparent fooling, asked his meaning; upon which Cottington replied that, "as the king's health depended upon his recreation, it was essential that the step should be taken." Laud, irritated beyond endurance by these flimsy sophistries, and blinded to their absurdity, flung from the room and went straight to the king to inveigh against Cottington, taking some pains to make his statements conclusive, and to discredit the Chancellor's pleas.

"My lord," said Charles, "you are deceived. Cottington is too hard for you. Upon my word, he hath not only dissuaded me more, and given more reasons against this business than all the men in England have done, but hath really obstructed the work by not doing his duty as I commanded him, for which I have been very much displeased with him. You see how unjustly your passion has transported you."

It is probable that Charles was too dependent on Laud, and too much moved by the evident warmth and enthusiasm for himself which had prompted these representations, to do more than administer the dignified rebuke above given. But it did not mend matters at Court—to have flung into the king's presence on a wild-goose chase, and to find that the man who fooled him was, after all, seriously on his side, was the kind of action that rankled in Laud's mind. He had no idea of people in high positions acting from spite or with double-facedness ; insincerity in the service of God and the king was unpardonable. And so he extended his disapproval to Cottington. In another man it would have been hatred. But Laud was not mean enough to hate ; he never condescended so far—it was too personal an action ; he merely disapproved on public grounds.

His style, both in speaking and writing, is terse and emphatic ; but it is not a good style. Occasionally it is too homely and humorous, as when, in one of his sermons at the Opening of Parliament, he says, speaking of some sinister prophecies about the future of the Church, "I cannot tell whether this be Balaam that prophesieth, or the Beast he rode on." He was not satisfied with his writing himself ; he published his sermons unwillingly, and by his will ordered many to be destroyed. Of his published speeches there are very few ; the best known is that delivered at the Star Chamber, on the occasion of Bastwick's censure. I subjoin a few extracts :—

"Reformers," he says, "are tolerable, if we are sure that they are patriots ; if not, if there is any self-seeking motive, there is no species so detestable.

"*Quis tulerit Gracchos ?* for it is apparent that the intention of these men is to raise a schism, being themselves as great incendiaries in the State as they have been in the Church.

"Worship," he says, "is set at nought."

"For my own part, I think myself bound to worship with Body as well as in Soul whenever I come where God is worshipped. And were this kingdom such as would allow no Holy Table standing in its proper place, yet I would worship God when I came into His house, and were the times such as should beat down churches, and all the curious and carven work thereof with axes and hammers, as in Ps. lxxiv. 6—and such times have been—yet would I worship in what place soever I came to pray, tho' there were not so much as a stone laid for Bethel. But this is the misery—'tis superstition nowadays for any man to come with more reverence into a church than a Tinker and his Bitch come into an Alehouse ; the Comparison is too homely, but my just indignation at the temper of the times makes me speak it.

"Reverence is due towards His altar, as the greatest place of God's residence here upon Earth. I say the greatest, yea, greater than the Pulpit, for there 'tis *Hoc est Corpus meum ;* but in the Pulpit 'tis at most *Hoc est Verbum meum,* and a greater reverence no doubt is due to the Body than to the Word of God. And so in relation answerably to the Throne, where his Body is usually present, than to the Seat whence his Word useth to be proclaimed."

The sermons that remain to us, such as the little volume published in ᵉ1651, are curiously difficult reading; they are closely argued, emphatically stated, but have not the quality of permanence. I know of no reading where the attention so persistently wanders and is so rarely enchained. The whole matter and style of controversy is utterly alien from our own. They are mainly on unity, on the pre-rogatives of authority, and kindred subjects, crab-bedly discussed. It is not nowadays sufficient, to recommend political principles, that they should be found to stand on an Old Testament basis ; a verse of the Psalms is not sufficient to stamp

a Parliamentary enactment as sound.   But this
was different when the House of Commons was
not the "honourable" but the "godly" House, and
when members spoke with Bibles in their hands
and made a copious commentary of texts.

. His speech in reply to a harangue of "sour
divinity" from Lord Saye and Sele on the abolition
of Episcopacy, and his controversy with Fisher,
the Jesuit, belong to the same class of literature.
They are justly forgotten.

For Laud was not one of those minds that win
an influence over all generations by the breadth of
their grasp, by their aloofness from all local and
temporary considerations ; he rather owed his
strength to his concentratedness, to his exact
adaptation to the position he held.   Minds are of
two classes, general and special.   As the historical
student comes across traces of the general mind,
his immediate feeling is, " How modern all this is ! "
This modernness has been attained by width of
view, by the largeness which is not at the mercy
of any surrounding circumstances or tendencies ;
and though such writings as these, and the thoughts
which they reflect, have an absorbing interest, yet
the actual life of such characters is apt to be
less interesting.   They were too great, too liberal,
to abandon themselves to the controversies of a

particular age ; from petty differences they turned
with weariness, because they had gazed upon truth
in its bewildering height and clearness.

Now the lives of those who fitted very closely
into the history of their own epoch, are apt to lose
interest if isolated from their immediate surroundings. Thus those of Laud's writings which deal
with general subjects have forfeited nearly all their
value. It is when he comes into close contact with
the great movements and great personages of the
time that he instantly absorbs our attention.

Among the most interesting of the Laudian papers
at Lambeth are a number of annual Reports on the
ecclesiastical condition of his province, addressed
to the king. They are written in various hand-
writings, never in the Archbishop's own, but always
signed by him. They begin on January 2, 1633.

Interesting for two reasons—Firstly, on account
of the trivialities with which they deal. Any one
would expect a report of this nature to be detailed ;
but these, from their shortness, cannot be exhaustive,
though they treat of recalcitrant lecturers, non-
residence of bishops, ruinous churches, criminous
clerks, and much other small business. They are
very business-like documents, very different from
the reports sent in by Laud's predecessor, the
dreary paragraphs of which all begin with the same

formula, " For aught I know." That was not Laud's
line ; there was nothing in his province that he did
not either know or feel himself bound to know.

But the real interest of the collection centres in
the fact that every one of these reports has been
oculis submissa fidelibus. The king read them
all, and, what is more, annotated them. In his tall
fine hand, with his exceedingly erratic spelling, he
has scribbled upon these documents and initialled
them.

For instance, in Laud's report of Lichfield and
Coventry, the following entry occurs :—

" The Lecturer went from Village to Village, and
at the end of the week proclaimed where they
should hear him next, that his Disciples might
follow : they say that this Lecturer is ordained to
illuminate the Dark Corners of the Diocese."

Against this the king has written (I give the
original spelling)—

" *If ther bee darke Corners in this Dioces, it were
fitt a trew light should illuminat it, and not by this
that is falce and uncertaine.*—C. R."
And again—

" *What the H. C.* [High Commission] *cannot doe
in this, I shall supply in a more powerful way.*"
And—

" *Lett him goe, wee ar well ridd of him.*"

And—

"*Try your way for some time.*"

And—

"*It is most fitt.*"

And—

"*Herein I shall not fail to do my part.*"

And—

"*I shall doe so.   Call for them.*"

"*Demande their helpe ; if they refuse I shall make them assist you.*"

At the end of one he writes—

"*I hope it is to be understoode that what is not certefied not to be amiss is right, tuching the obser- vation of my instructions: that granted this is no ill Certificat.*

"*Feb.* 16$\frac{39}{40}$.   *C. R.*"

These are such characteristic comments, so self-willed and authoritative ; and it was so characteristic of the king to annotate—he did it on all his books and papers. It is wonderfully interesting to turn over these originals, to see the actual papers that stood for so much, and the traces of the thoughts of busy minds. I do not think that anything in my researches gave me such a thrill of pleasure as this little discovery : it confirms so admirably the impression of the detailed and

paternal working of the whole institution ; it recalls
the days when kings had the disposition and the
leisure to busy themselves about unlicensed lecturers
at Coventry, and the position of the altar, and the
sale of Puritan tracts.   We can hardly wonder
that Laud, backed with these marks of royal confidence and esteem, held his fatal progress with
scarcely a misgiving.   That his Dread Sovereign,
like himself, was doomed to fall, was a dream too
fantastic to visit even that foreboding brain.

But of all Laud's remains the famous Diary is
by far the most interesting.   It is quite by an
accident that it was made public.   There is no
doubt, I think, that he would have made away
with it if he had known that it was to be handled
and selected by Prynne ; even, I believe, if he had
suspected that it was ever to see the light.   And for
this very reason it deserves a very tender handling.
It is a collection of miscellaneous jottings of all
kinds ; anything which struck him as being of interest
he appears to have entered—memoranda of public
events, very private entries, even mere unintelligible facts about his health, his dreams, his adventures of every kind—but all meant for his own
perusal, and for no other eye.   That was not the
age when a public man might look forward, as is
the deplorable fashion now, with tolerable certainty

to the editing of his diaries and letters with copious notes.

It is hard indeed to see any motive in such a compilation, for it is evidently not put together for purposes of business—it is far too miscellaneous and casual; he must have scribbled down somewhat whimsically anything that struck him. It is, as a consequence, full of mannerisms, and gives the best possible picture, because it is so unconscious, of the man.

Thus it is a strange book, of wonderful interest, as the secret record of a very enigmatic mind. It was an age of ciphers. The notorious "thorough" which is so frequently found in his letters to Strafford and in Strafford's replies is a sign of this. "Thorough" stood, as has been said, for some sweeping policy which they had discussed together and bound themselves to carry out. But, besides this, in the Diary there are constantly occurring mysterious initials, the key to which has never been found. Prynne's interpretation is characteristic; he professes to see in them the record of clandestine and immoral intimacies. This is, of course, nothing more than a defamation.

So far is clear. He seems to note his first meeting with certain people, and the various stages of their intimacy. "There I first knew what E. H.

thought of me." " Hope was given to me of A. H.,
Jan. 1, which afterwards proved my great happiness.
I begin to hope it, Jan. 21. My next infortunate-
ness was with E. B., Dec. 30. A stay in this.
My great business with E. B. began Jan. 22. It
settled as it could, March 5. It hath had many
changes, and what will become of it God knoweth."

It is strangely superstitious too. He remarks
how often he is falling upon the day of " Decollation of St. John Baptist." He notes such facts as
two robins flying into his study, his nose bleeding
(a rare occurrence), his picture slipping from the
wall, and many other trivial incidents—why, we
cannot quite divine,—perhaps it was an early habit
unconsciously contracted and never overcome, of
thinking of little events as portents. The well-
known parallel of Dr. Johnson will occur to every
mind ; he rebukes himself for mentioning such
things, and excuses himself humorously on the
ground that he has been accustomed to do so.

Those writers whose enthusiasm for Laud is
highest have dwelt much upon the devotional side
of his character. They speak of the buried life of
prayer as being his real life, that in which he moved
most easily, that to which he gratefully returned
in the intervals of business, as a jewel which he
took out to gaze upon in secret.

This rests upon some rather exaggerated expression of remorse in the Diary, some hints of his great delight in the Church Service, his book of private devotions, and little more. But in the Diary the devotional expressions bear a most microscopic proportion to the secular entries ; and any candid student must confess that the Devotions are far more liturgical than devotional. It is not the mystic who writes his prayers out in a book. The precision of such an arrangement is thoroughly antagonistic to the vaguer and more spontaneous impulses of contemplation. No! the man who has his volume of private prayer is rather the soul who feels the need of the frequent cleansing of prayer, and at the same time is conscious of the difficulty of attaining his end without some extraneous help and appointed form.

I do not think we are justified in saying more than that he was a prayerful man, but more liturgically prayerful than contemplatively. I do not think that he went to his prayers for light and leading (the one extract that I have given, p. 12, is of too practical a kind), but that he looked upon them as a bounden duty and as a source of comfort. I am sure that his secular life was far more real to him than the meditative life could possibly have been.

Lastly, his dreams. Of these he makes constant mention. " Dreamed that all the teeth of my lower jaw fell out save one, which I had much ado to hold in with both my hands." " Dreamed that my mother shewed me a certain old man; he seemed to lie upon the ground—merry enough, but with a wrinkled countenance. His name was Grove." At one time it was always about Williams. " Dreamed that the L.ᵈ K. [Keeper], was dead : that I passed by one of his men that was about a monument for him : that I heard him say that his lower lip was infinitely swelled and fallen, and he rotten already. This dream did trouble me." " In my sleep his Majesty King J. appeared to me [this was after his death]. I saw him only passing by swiftly. He was of a pleasant and serene countenance. In passing he saw me and beckoned to me, smiled, and was immediately withdrawn from my sight.

" Sep. 26, Sunday. That night I dreamed of the marriage of I know not whom at Oxford. All that were present were clothed in flourishing green garments. I knew none of them, but Thomas Flaxnye. Immediately after, without any intermission of sleep (that I know of), I thought I saw the Bishop of Worcester, his head and shoulders covered with linen. He advised and invited me

kindly to dwell with them, marking out a place
where the Court of Marches of Wales was then
held. But not staying for my answer, he subjoined, that he knew I could not live so meanly, etc.

"My dream of my Blessed Lord and Saviour,
J. C., one of the most comfortable passages that
I ever had in my life."

These are not important facts, but they are
characteristic. In constructing historical portraits,
we cannot afford to sacrifice any point, however
small. They only confirm the notion of the busy
mind, never resting even during sleep, turning over
and over in that grotesque image-land the capital
it has gained in the day.

CHAPTER XIV.

THERE is one question closely connected with the life and principles of Laud which deserves especial consideration, bearing as it does so nearly upon the controversy which, consciously or unconsciously, is at the root of so much of the religious dissidence of modern days.

The most ardent religious reformers of the present time are perhaps to be found in the school that attaches the highest possible value to the form and ritual of worship. The Ritualists have established their claim to serious consideration by the notable success which attends their evangelistic efforts. Among the poorest populations of large towns, that class which political philosophers tell us contains the already germinating seeds of our future rulers, the Democracy, they labour unceasingly, and their labours are not in vain. It seems at present as if the only great successes which have been recorded in the attempts to evangelize the masses have been attained by one or the other of two great movements—the internal and the external.

The internal movement has been that of Dissent. General Booth, whose sympathetic knowledge of the wants of these bewildering millions has been won by an inner acquaintance, through birth and training, with these needs, represents perhaps most adequately the most vigorous attempt that has been made, so to speak, *within* the lower classes to raise themselves spiritually. Mr. Moody has done the same for the middle class. They have had, and continue to have, their successes ; their converts are numbered by tens of thousands.

The external movement has been numerically even more successful, though conducted in a wider and less concentrated manner. The Ritualists have engaged successfully in the great war against the lower nature of mankind when forced into its most depraved luxuriance by the poisonous atmosphere of our great cities.

The Socialists who have attempted the same task have failed, because they have supposed that a material solution of these problems is possible. It is clear to any one who has seen and studied the axioms of the case that nothing is possible but a spiritual elevation.

The Ritualists have come to the conflict armed

with despised, but none the less potent weapons.
They have thought no influence too high for the
task. They have brought to the very poorest, forms
of mysterious antiquity, suggestions of truth couched
in the most mystical terms, ancient treasures of
art and music, movement and culture ; and these
things have been effective?

And yet these practices are of a kind which are
said to make the ordinary English layman " stamp "
with impatience when he witnesses them or hears
them described, at their extravagance, their petti-
ness, their pretension. He cannot bring himself
to believe that a system which is based upon so
much that is antique and mannerized, that clings
so close to precedent and rule, that is so precise
and formal, can be anything but ludicrous and
unworthy of the Christian simplicity. And yet,
if he will look patiently at results, he must resist
that contemptuous impulse. He may say, of
course, that it is not the ritual, but the character
of the men that is effectual : but this is only trans-
ferring the problem to another ground. It must
be made clear why men of such essential purity
and goodness cling so close to and regard as so
vital and potent these ceremonial appliances.

All attempts to bridge the gulf have failed. Broad
rational systems have melted into air. The

teaching of Maurice and Kingsley, once so gloriously hopeful, is 'recognized to be hopelessly unsatisfying. Unitarianism, even under Dr. Martineau, only attacks the balanced intellect, and effects few conquests there. Positivism is confined to a few refined thinkers. The constant outcry to liberalize Church dogma has done nothing. There is no *media via* possible.

On the one hand there is the vehement accusation that truth is clouded over with forms ; that it is not life but Formalism ; that the essentials have been overlaid with adventitious by-play ; that justice has disappeared in the tithing of mint, and truth is confused with anise. What spirituality, it is said, can be found in a Creed which maintains in the face of Science the resurrection of the body, and holds the institution of Episcopacy to be nearly Divine ?

On the other hand it is retorted that if the symbolic form be lost the truth perishes too ; that human nature is so weak that it needs material reminders : that if they are Formalists, Christ was a Formalist too ; that He laid down close rules of ecclesiastical procedure, and guided with His Spirit the nascent Church that developed them into an organization.

Laud's position was the latter. He had no

patience with iconoclasts.   He enjoined the absolute necessity of outward reverence upon humanity.
Compounded as we are, he said, of gross material
and spiritual insight, the flesh must prostrate
itself at the bidding of the spirit when it finds
itself in the presence of the great One of the
spiritual kingdom.   But it cannot be doubted that
he held so fast to the form that the spirit was
partly blurred.   If we could trace in his work the
spirit of ardent social reform, of absorbing anxiety
for the communication of spiritual truth, we might
have forgiven him ; but this we cannot discern.

It seems strange that he should have imagined
himself, without misgiving, to be treading closely
in the steps of that Master Who took His sacraments
from the commonest and most ordinary acts of
material life—eating and washing,—Who spoke of
the coming dissolution of all local worship, "not
at Jerusalem nor in this mountain," of the ceremonial freedom which awaited men.   No rational
thinker can help feeling that the institution of a
ceremonial tyranny in that Name, to do that more
than human spirit honour, is one of the cruellest
ironics that has ever befallen the human race.   No
one can read the gospel with unbiassed eyes and
not avow this.

"Should   not   the   life   be   the   sacrifice?"   was

asked by an eager unsatisfied searcher after truth, of one of the greatest living exponents of Christian truth. "Yes," was the answer; "but where is the hymn and the incense? where are the white garments of the priest?"

May I be excused for here inserting a letter on this immediate text, from a living Churchman, who will be allowed by most to speak with authority upon the subject? It seems to me to represent so nearly what Laud would have wished to say, had he possessed the idealizing power, the gift of poetical expression, that I cannot feel it to be beside the mark.

"As to public worship, I think that there is real depth in what Mr. —— said in his enigmatic way. Besides the Life and Self (which cannot be *offered* perhaps in a real sense except by union with outward elements—just as Our Lord placed His humanity in union with our life and the life of our species for this among other purposes)— besides Life and Self we surely ought to present not only what we are, but what we have for a time— the things which in this world our spirit or self is allowed to possess, εἰς χρῆσιν, for use, and which it will have to lay down. Of all these, the results and the instruments of Art are the ἄνθος, the flower, and those results which exist and pass, are born and die, are the subtlest and most delicate and perfect. And those also which have an image of eternity about them are at the other pole of perfectness. Form, colour, order, movement have somehow to be offered as well as thought. Even that which is ours only instantaneously — Time —must have its consecration too, through the dedicating of certain intervals to the Service of God.

"Drop that for a minute.

"The yearning (which is so undeniable in all men) for God requires *speech*. The roughest and rudest come together to speak to God. In their plainest way He speaks to them, and they know it.

"When they are delivered, or are being delivered from material terms with regard to Him, only the best persevere (those in whom the yearning is, as I say, for God and not for comfort) in following out what they find—namely, that the listening to the records of His revelation through ages, and the substance of it, and the speaking in common to Him, and exhorting one another about the hindrances in getting to Him, and the seeking His hand in difficulties, affect their lives more than anything else does. This simplest, plainest worship in common strengthens as well as reminds them to rededicate their lives and spirits to Him. Nothing can eradicate the conviction—the experimental conviction they all entertain—that it is not the exercise of the worship, but an undoubted answer made to their worship which is the strength. They sought a Presence, and they have found it. Surely they are not wrong in gathering that what obtains so gracious an answer is acceptable to the Answerer —a sweet-smelling savour—ὀσμὴ εὐδοκίας.

"Now, as Life becomes more beautiful in this sensuous region, the question comes, '*Is this a new world we have found for ourselves? Is it a region into which we shall enter, and do without God there? Or is it capable of being sanctified like all else we have known in plainer ways?*' There is a trembling about the question. But surely it has been rightly answered, and the dedication of all those perfect-nesses is lawful and right. And the glory of Art goes up to Him from those who have it for use, εἰς χρῆσιν, and the appropriateness, the εὐδοκία of it, is in the very nature of things.

"But now, I own, I have for years past looked on pleased but anxious to see our worship all over England getting ornamental. The white garments and the chanting and the windows trouble me with a strange trouble while I hope all is well. I can explain by an almost ridiculous thing. I can't endure to use a Psalter with notes to every syllable.

I become as if I were chanting Vedas. I fear that I shall come to think that we don't *know* that what we do is acceptable, except that we can't find out what else to do than what is actually in man to do.

"For ourselves, I believe the only thing is to throw consciousness into all; to fling up, before each attempt at an elaborate piece of service, before even each change of chant, before each sitting down even to practise at the organ, the thought, 'This is Thine, O Lord: of Thee, in Thee: O make it also for Thee.'"

CHAPTER XV.

IN reviewing shortly the problems suggested by such a life and death, we must first consider what claims are made for him and the value of his work by his most ardent admirers. "The English Church," they say, "is, in its Catholic aspect, a memorial of Laud." This is a considerable claim. When we ask how this is supported, they begin by saying that we owe the retention of Episcopacy in the Church to him. The causal connection, if there be one, is intricate. Episcopacy was abolished in Laud's lifetime, and was resumed as a matter of course when the monarchical and Tory reaction against Puritanism set in. But I venture to maintain that it was not by any means Laud's memory which consecrated the thought of Episcopacy to its restorers, as Charles's memory undoubtedly consecrated monarchy. On the contrary, I believe that it was almost entirely due to Laud's personal unpopularity that Episcopacy was so summarily

abolished ; I believe it might have continued intact
through the Rebellion but for him. Let us press
Laud's supporters a little further. We ask if there
is anything else that we owe to Laud. They
answer, the Prayer Book. That assertion I again
conceive to rest on very much the same basis of
proof. It cannot be established. Last of all they
fall back triumphantly upon the position of the
altar in our churches. I confess that, though I
should deplore the alteration of that arrangement,
I cannot bring myself to be enthusiastic about it ;
it does not seem to be identical with the Catholic
aspect of the English Church. In fact, to attribute
to Laud the existence of that aspect, is as absurd
as to say that we owe our present monarchy to
Charles I. The manner of Charles's death created,
I think, a very enthusiastic detestation of the principles which sanctioned it, and so may be said to
have had an indirect effect ; but I do not believe
that even this can be asserted about Laud.

The fact is, we do not like to speak lightly about
a man who sealed his principles with his blood.
There is an unconscious reverence for devotion
that will flinch at nothing, not even the last passage,
of which we cannot and would not rid ourselves.
And when that devotion is founded on a mistaken
conception, such a death becomes one of the most

tragic and pathetic sketches that we can well see, but it is not necessarily inspiring : it arouses sympathy for the sufferer, none for the cause in which he is suffering.

And Laud's cause was not a true one. His ideal of the Church which he upheld falls far short of truth. He did not believe the Church to be an all-embracing society for holy living, the possessor of certain gracious thoughts and Divine influences, which cannot be exactly felt or received outside her bounding line. The freedom of the gospel was lost upon him. He chose to regard her as an essentially political organization, sister of the State. Her ecclesiastics were to be courtiers too ; she was to have her pageants and her days of observation, her high festivals and solemnities. In these he conceived some essence of her being to lie ; he did not look upon them as mere adjuncts of a huge human organization, which in the ideal society would find no place.

"I set upon the repair of the Material and Spiritual Church together," as Laud wrote to Strafford. This was his ideal for the Church. This is the question that keeps pressing itself home upon us as we look at the character of the efforts in which he so ceaselessly engaged. We see lecturers deprived, fonts repaired, altars railed off, surplices

enforced ; we find immense noisy activity : in the
centre there is a bustling eager figure, signing,
writing, scolding, confuting ;—and all the time a
terrible suspicion is creeping on us : "To what
purpose?" Clumsy and ugly as the Puritan methods
were, forfeiting as they did so much of their due
genuine influences by their contempt for externals,
yet these grim tiresome figures had *conduct* at heart.
And had Laud ? He would have affirmed it, undoubtedly ; but, looking at his work, can we feel
that his secret aspirations turned in that direction ?
Not honestly, I think. He worshipped externals ;
he was a Formalist. The Puritans were weakened
by their want of forms, for human nature must
have forms ; it desires them so eagerly : but a still
greater danger is waiting at the other end. It is
dangerous to be without them, but it is still more
dangerous to depend on them.

Let us hear what Heylyn, Laud's most uncritical
friend and admirer, has to say of the progress and
ideals of the Church under him.

"If we look," he says, "into the Church as it
stood under his Direction, we shall find the Prelates
generally more intent upon the work committed
to them, the Clergy joining together to advance the
work of Uniformity recommended to them, the
Liturgy more punctually executed in all the parts

and offices of it. The Word more diligently preached, the Sacraments more reverently administered than in some score of years before ; the people more Conformable to those Reverend Gestures in the House of God, which, though prescribed before, were but little practised ; more cost laid out upon the beautifying and adorning of Parochial Churches, in furnishing and repairing Parsonage Houses than in all the times since the Reformation ; the Clergy grown to such esteem, for parts and power, that the gentry thought none of their Daughters to be better disposed of, than such as they had lodged in the Arms of a Churchman ; and the Nobility grown so well affected to the state of the Church, that *some of them designed their younger sons* to the Order of Priesthood to make them capable of rising in the same Ascendant." What a climax ! Then follows a passage on Doctrine, praising " the Uniformity of teaching,. and the Piety and learning of her defenders." The word " piety" is but once mentioned in the passage. It is too much like the reports on which we build our ideas of Church progress nowadays—so many churches built, so many communicants, so much money subscribed. Of course vast subscription lists are indicative of a spirit of much willingness to sacrifice material goods to secure the Church's material prosperity; but if these are the lines which her chief pastors lay down for her advance, is not the flock deluded after all? And is not Laud's life an instance of this? Look at his most private thoughts. If the heart be set on character-ideals, on the simplification of the issues of life, and accepts the material organization as a convenient substratum of possibilities, then the true hopes will break out somewhere—in letters, in sermons, in recorded speech. This does not appear in Laud. On the Church's material greatness his mind was set; to this his secret aspirations turned; after this the fervent longings of his spirit went out. State and Church, two fair sisters hand-in-hand, were to relieve the nation of all independent thought, of all individual wishes, of all private ventures after happiness: public happiness was to be secured on a large public scale. Government, Rule—not self-government, the will of the people—were his sacred words. Authority, Tradition—these the people were to follow, paying such due reverence at the shrines, as God had appointed, and as the historical issues of worship had modified. This was Laud's dream. It was a splendid vision; only do not let us make the mistake of thinking or calling it a religious one.

By zeal for this great institution, by passionate

love for her traditions, by blind prejudice for her methods, Laud rose and fell ; not a single thought of self mingled with the devotion with which he served her. If the three mysterious temptations of our Saviour correspond to the stages of trial through which human leaders pass, Laud may be said to have passed safely through the first two, but to have succumbed to the last. He did not use the power within him to gratify luxurious tastes ; he did not use it to surround himself with an atmosphere of peculiar honour ; but, when confronted with the temptation to have recourse to lower earthly weapons for the establishment of a spiritual kingdom, he was blinded there and fell.

To be a hero it is not enough to be true—a man must also be tender : to have no taint of self, or selfish aims, is not enough. There must be a deliberate extension of sympathy to others. Laud's ideal was a high one, but it was too hardly, too militantly, too unsympathetically held. He never thought it a duty to examine the treasured ideals of others ; he never for an instant had even the curiosity to regard life from another point of view. In ordinary life it was the same. He had no friends. He had some faithful dependants who served him well—Heylyn and Hyde ; some strong political allies who admired—as who does not ?—

the tremendous fibre and force of such a nature : but of the depth and delicacy that attract and retain equal outspoken friendships, he had none. Of all great churchmen he is the only one who had not even female admirers.

And therefore we reluctantly confess that, in an age of heroes, a stage crowded with heroic figures, Laud is not among them. Pym and Strafford, Buckingham and Cromwell, these are men indeed. Not so Laud, not his luckless master. As head of a great Christian society, he was so strangely un-Christlike : ready enough with the scourge of small cords, he showed no mercy to those who made their gains out of the sanctuary ; but neither had he love for the poor crowds outside. He could pull down, but not build up.

The great mistake, indeed, that the three martyrs made was this : they were not great enough to grasp the beauty of feeling with the popular mind, nor enlightened enough to see the necessity for it. They misunderstood and miscalculated the force of the democracy. They clapped the valves down, so that when roaring and tumultuous the irrepressible strength streamed out, wantoning in all the consciousness of newly discovered might, the three champions of repression were struck down.

If they were sincere, it is well with them ; they

were blest if they did it faithfully. For we must remember that seekers after truth are but as men wandering on a sphere; though they strike away from some, from any point, with faces averted and backs rigidly turned, let them only move straight forward and they will meet again upon some unknown pole.

A LIST OF LAUD'S PREFERMENTS.

1593. Fellow of St. John's.

1603. Chaplain to the Earl of Devonshire.

1607. Vicar of Stanford (Northampton).

1608. Rector of North Kilworth (Leicestershire), and chaplain to Neile, Bishop of Rochester.

1609. North Kilworth exchanged for West Tilbury, in Essex.

1610. Fellowship resigned. Vicar of Cuchstone (Kent), exchanged in the same year for Vicarage of Norton.

1611. President of St. John's. Chaplain to the King.

1614. Prebendary of Bugden, in Lincoln Cathedral.

1615. Archdeacon of Huntingdon, in Lincoln Cathedral.

1616. Dean of Gloucester, resigned West Tilbury.

1617. Vicar of Ibstock (Leicestershire); resigned Norton.

1620. Prebendary of Westminster.

1621. Bishop of St. David's; resigned Presidentship of St. John's.

1622. Vicar of Creeke.

1625. Resigned Ibstock. Bishop of Bath and Wells.

1628. Bishop of London.

1633. Archbishop of Canterbury.

PRINTED BY WILLIAM CLOWES AND SONS, LIMITED, LONDON AND BECCLES.